# SCRAP

To Ruth
For always coming with me
(Especially to the emporium)
~ GB

To my Love, friends and family,
who are the source of my inspiration and motivation.
Thank you for being part of my journey
~ AT

LITTLE TIGER
An imprint of Little Tiger Press Limited
1 Coda Studios, 189 Munster Road,
London SW6 6AW

Imported into the EEA by Penguin Random House Ireland,
Morrison Chambers, 32 Nassau Street, Dublin D02 YH68

www.littletiger.co.uk

A paperback original
First published in Great Britain in 2023
Text copyright © Guy Bass, 2023
Illustrations copyright © Alessia Trunfio, 2023

ISBN: 978-1-78895-597-3

The right of Guy Bass and Alessia Trunfio to be identified as the author and illustrator of this
work respectively has been asserted by them in accordance with the Copyright, Designs and
Patents Act, 1988.

A CIP catalogue record for this book is available from the British Library.

Printed and bound in the UK.

The Forest Stewardship Council® (FSC®) is a global, not-for-profit organization dedicated to
the promotion of responsible forest management worldwide. FSC defines standards based on
agreed principles for responsible forest stewardship that are supported by environmental, social,
and economic stakeholders. To learn more, visit www.fsc.org

10 9 8 7 6 5 4 3 2 1

# SCRAP

## GUY BASS

### ILLUSTRATED BY ALESSIA TRUNFIO

**LiTTLE TiGER**

LONDON

*Not All Robots Are Created Equal.*

*From* Memoir of a Mechanical Mayor *by Harmony Highshine*

# A BRIEF HISTORY OF SOMEWHERE

By Natalie 'Gnat' Brightside, Aged 11 ½

This isn't my story, but I'm the only human left to tell it.

I wasn't there for the first part, mainly 'cause I hadn't been born yet.

The year was Something Something. Humans had spread like peanut butter across the galaxy, looking for new planets to call Somewhere.

One of those planets was *Somewhere 513*.

That one, the little one.

I know – it doesn't look like much.

Sometimes big stories come in small packages.

With new planets, you always send in the robots first. Servants with servos, loyal to the core, programmed to prepare the planet for humanity's arrival. Give them time and they can turn an alien wasteland into Somewhere not bad at all. And that's exactly what they did. They even built a whole city, and got it all nice for the humans' arrival.

But this time something happened that hadn't happened before. The robots sort of got to *like* the city they'd built. They got to like the little back-of-beyond world called Somewhere 513.

I guess it started to feel like home.

When the humans finally showed up, all bleary-eyed from space-sleep, they couldn't wait to make themselves at home on their world. But by then the robots had done something that robots had never done before.

They'd decided to keep it.

Keep it? said the humans. What do you mean?

It means, we've had a change of core, the robots said. The planet belongs to us now.

Uh, OK, said the humans. You'll still do everything we ask though, right? You'll do all the work – all the lifting and carrying and toiling and suchlike?

Actually, the robots said, we're not doing any of that.

Huh, said the humans. Will you still make us breakfast?

Especially not breakfast, said the robots. It's horrible watching you eat. Especially knowing how it all ends up. No, we're not doing anything for you any more.

Fair enough, said the humans. So what time are you serving breakfast?

I don't know if anyone really got what was happening until it had already happened. But pretty soon after that, being human was outlawed on Somewhere 513. The robots ordered the humans to leave the planet altogether – but Somewhere 513 was a long way from anywhere. Sometimes when you're Somewhere, you have nowhere else to go.

That was when the fighting started. The robots called it the Difference of Opinion ... but you'd probably call it war. Humans vs Robots. Actually, more like one hundred humans vs one thousand robots. The humans wouldn't have stood a chance except for one thing ... and that thing was K1-NG.

One robot. One single robot actually fought to protect the humans. K1-NG stood against his fellow machines, one robot against a thousand. He fought cog and nail, and he never gave up. Not even when he knew he couldn't win ... not even when he sacrificed himself so that the humans could escape. Even then, even when he was battered and broken and beaten, he never gave up. Deep down, at his core, K1-NG was unstoppable.

OK, *nearly* unstoppable. See, in the end, it wasn't the

robots who defeated K1-NG. It was the humans.

They did something to K1-NG he could never forgive. They betrayed him … betrayed everything he'd fought for. On that day K1-NG finally gave up. He vowed never to fight for another human being as long as he lived.

So I suppose this is his story. The story of K1-NG.

The humans called him King of the Robots.

I called him Scrap.

# THE PILE

*Going Somewhere?*
*At the Fargone Corporation, your future is our priority.*
*Let Fargone take you on a journey through the stars to a brighter future –*
*and with over 1,000 dedicated, hard-working robots preparing the planet for your*
*arrival, we're confident you'll feel at home from the moment you arrive.*
*Reach the foregone conclusion with the Fargone Corporation –*
*Your new Somewhere is waiting for you!*

**From Your Guide to a New Somewhere**
**By the Fargone Corporation**

On the Pile, the one and a half suns could never set soon enough.

Every day was the same. The robot woke with the dawn upon his small patch of junk. Among the small mountains of debris before him he saw ruined robot parts – limbs ... heads ... torsos ... even whole bodies ... decimated robot *cases*. These cases piled up in their hundreds, their chest cavities open and empty, motionless and inert without their life-giving cores.

The robot watched the Pile's other residents – junk

cases – rusting robots on their last metal legs, trying to make the best of a miserable existence. He watched them build crude houses out of cast-offs, and call them homes.

But the robot did nothing.

He just sat there and waited for his core to run out of charge.

It never did.

Even though he saw countless junk cases grind to a halt, he did not lose an ounce of power. Not a single ounce. For the robot's core had been built to last, like a battery that never ran out ... a heart that never stopped beating. He was never going to fade away, as he had hoped.

So he watched the suns set again.

And again, and again.

On the eve of his tenth year on the Pile, the robot woke up with the dawn and stared out as normal. Makeshift shacks now dotted the landscape. The robot had watched dozens of junk cases build humble homes and humbler lives, before unceremoniously running out of charge. The robot looked back at his empty patch and realized something had changed. He realized he was tired of waiting to fade away.

He didn't want just to be there.

He wanted to *belong* there.

It took the robot a full month to build his house, a ramshackle cabin made from leftover parts even the junk cases didn't want. But as he chiselled the word WELCOME on to a sheet of battered tin and laid it outside his front door, he realized that he had made himself a home.

A week later, as he furnished his home with the final piece of improvised furniture, he realized he had given himself a small sense of belonging.

And a week after that, as he tended the flower bed in his tiny front garden, the robot realized that for the first time since he had arrived on the Pile, he had not thought about humans. It seemed he had finally found a way to leave the past behind.

For that he was eternally grateful.

"It's him," said a voice. The robot dropped his trowel and spun round. Silhouetted in the glare of one and a half setting suns stood two figures. They were no more than a metre away – one slightly taller than he was, the other a little shorter. Their bodies were covered by thick, pocket-ridden ponchos. Hoods pulled over their heads cast dark shadows over their faces. One had a large satchel strung across their chest. A small power battery poked out of the top.

*Junk cases*, thought the robot.

"This is -zk- my patch," he said, gesturing back at his house. "Get lost."

"It's not him," said tall.

"Is too," short replied.

"Can't be."

"Can too."

"But *look* at him."

"Exactly, we finded him."

"Found."

The short one turned back to the robot. "You *are* him, aren't you?"

"Who are -zk- *you*?" the robot stuttered. Short lowered her hood.

The tall one shouted, "Wait!" but the robot had already seen her face. He stumbled backwards, suddenly weak at the knees, and fell, rump first, into his flower bed. He stared up in horror, hardly able to believe his eyes.

Human.

A human child.

Which was impossible.

Because there were no humans on Somewhere 513.

Tall lowered her hood then too.

Another human.

"How…?" he gasped. "What -zk- who are—"

"I'm Gnat and that's Paige," interrupted short. "Gnat". Brownish skin. Reddish hair. 5.7 years old. Grubby. Missing central incisor. 60% water. "We came to find you," Gnat continued. She prodded at the gap in her teeth. "We had a little moon-buggy but we crashed it on the first day and my tooth fell out but it was loose anyway and we walked the rest of the way on our feet and now is now, and we've find – founded you."

"I'm telling you, this isn't him," said tall. "Paige". Much the same as short, but older. 10.3? No, 10.4. Less grubby, no less scruffy. Strangely familiar. 100% impossible. She pulled her poncho off her arm and inspected a metallic armguard fixed to her left wrist. "Tracer must've conked out," she added with a tut.

The robot shook with disbelief. He had hoped never to see another human face again … hoped never to be reminded of the life he had lost – of the robot he once was.

Yet here were two of them, watching him expectantly.

"You -zk- can't be…" the robot whispered, staring up at them. The light from his left eye flickered slightly and he wondered if faulty wiring could be causing him to hallucinate. "No -zk- way," he added. "You can't be real."

"Can too," replied Gnat, her gap-toothed smile wide and delighted. "Paige, tell him we're real."

"Let's go," said Paige, peering at the robot. "It *can't* be him."

"Him who?" asked the robot.

"It's *so* him," insisted Gnat with a gleeful grin.

"But look at him," said Paige. "He's *junk*."

"Hey!" snapped the robot. "That's -zk- *our* word. You don't get to say that word."

"No offence," said Paige with a shake of her head. "But also, seriously, look at you."

The robot looked down at his hands. They were spindly and dull and creaked with rust. He ran his fingers across his simple approximation of a face, little more than a pair of eyes and a small, hinged mouth, and then regarded his body, a battered, grey cylinder covered in rust, dings and dents. His legs didn't seem to belong to his body, nor to each other. His right was yellowish, with two pistons and a wide, flat foot, while the left was spindly and dull and had no foot at all, ending in a simple metal rod. There was no doubt he was the most downgraded robot on the Pile. Even among the junk cases, he was an unimposing sight.

"I know what I look like," he huffed.

"Don't listen to her – *I* think you look nifty. You're all bits and pieces," said Gnat. She nodded to herself and added, "I'm going to call you 'Scrap'."

"No, you're not," insisted the robot. With a tinny whirr, he managed to get to his feet, tottering unsteadily like a newborn calf.

"What's it *like* being a robot, actually?" asked Gnat, peering at him. "Do you get hot and cold 'cause I'm *always* hot, and does your brain think one thing or one million things because I think one thing or two things but that is *it* and I'd *definitely* like to be an actual robot. I'd be like you –" she leaned in and added, as if to remind the robot what she had done for him – "but not called Scrap 'cause that's *your* name."

"That is *not* my -zk- name," insisted the robot.

"So what *is* your name?" asked Paige bluntly.

The robot paused. He hadn't spoken his name in ten years. Indeed, he had vowed never again to speak it aloud.

"Doesn't matter what my name is," the robot grunted, jabbing his rusty chest with a rustier finger. "You can't just go around namin' folk."

"Why not?" asked Gnat.

"'Cause you can't."

"Why not?"

"Because you can't!" Scrap snapped. "Names are -zk- important."

"Sorry," said Gnat. Then she turned to Paige and added in a loud whisper, "*I bet he's called Scrap.*"

The robot let out a grunt and looked around.

"Might as -zk- well be…" he sighed, unaware that, from that moment, he would forever be known as Scrap. "Just a good-for-nothin' junk case…"

"Junk case?" Paige repeated.

"This *body* – if I was any more downgraded, I'd be nothin' but rust and dust," the robot replied. "There's nothin' on the Pile that's in a worst state than me. Trust me, I'm not the 'bot you're looking— Wait, *who are you*? You're… Humans are outlawed on Somewhere 513. What are you gubs even doin' here?"

"Founding you," replied Gnat. "We need your help."

"Me? Why?"

"Why do you think?" said Gnat as if the answer was obvious. "You're King of the Robots."

## EPISODE 02

# THE HUMANS

## Welcome to Somewhere 513
## All Are Welcome to Our Welcoming World
## See Exceptions*

*All non-humans remain welcome, including, without exception, indigenous life forms (extant / dormant / protean) transient or immigrant interplanetary alien visitation, and cosmic or cross-dimensional mass migration (organisms, microbes or biomass).

Just No Humans.

"What did you say?"

The words echoed around Scrap's head – memories of a life he had tried hard to forget sparked and fizzed in his brain-frame.

*King of the Robots.*

No one had called him that for ten years.

"I said," replied Gnat, "you're King of the—"

"Gnat, for the last time, it's not him," snapped Paige, grabbing her sister's arm. "Does he look like a king of *anything* to you?"

"Maybe he's changed – when it was ten years ago, you wore nappies and smelled like nappies." Gnat tutted at her sister before turning back to Scrap. "Do you know Dandelion Brightside?"

"Gnat!" Paige hissed.

Scrap felt his core run cold. That name. *That name*.

He peered at the humans, and immediately realized it was *her* he was seeing in them. How could he have missed it? It was in their searching dark eyes, their defiance, their will, their *hope*. It was their mother he saw. Their mother, who he had tried so hard not to think about for ten long years, might as well have been staring him in the face. In an instant his brain-frame was flooded with memories. The last day he saw her, and all the things he had said on that day, that he didn't regret – he *didn't*. He remembered leaving. He remembered her calling after him. He'd somehow always thought that, despite everything, they had managed to find a way off-world … that someone had come looking for them … that someone had sent help … that they had been rescued … that they had blasted off into the void and escaped this unforgiving, doomed Somewhere.

But it looked like they'd stayed, all this time.

And they'd had children.

"Our mum made you!" Gnat proudly declared. As Scrap gazed open-mouthed at the humans, Gnat helpfully mouthed her mother's name: "*Dan-dee-lion Bright-side.*"

"I -zk- I—" he blurted.

"Wait, *do* you know her?" asked Paige.

"What? Uh, no. No, I -zk- don't," he lied. With a rust-rasping shrug, he added, "I just heard the -zk- name, that's all. Dandelion Brightside designed the cores of every 'bot on Five One Three."

"And she made the magic glove that founded you," explained Gnat. "Abradadadadabra!"

"That's not the word – and it's *not* a magic glove," huffed Paige as she tapped her armguard. It was made from a dull orange metal, and mounted upon it was what looked like a compass together with a small screen filled with blinking lights. "It's a core tracer," she added impatiently. "It's for—"

"I know what a core tracer is," Scrap interrupted.

"Mum said it would find the King of the Robots," said Gnat. For clarification she added, "That's you. King of the—"

"Stop sayin' that!" Scrap snapped. He cast his eyes across the Pile. Other junk cases, not a hundred paces away, were beginning to pay attention to Scrap's new visitors. "Now you listen to me – you can't be -zk- out here," Scrap hissed. "Humans are outlawed on Somewhere Five One Three. You need to go home and *hide*."

"We can't," said Paige, pulling her hood back over her head before nudging her sister to do the same. "Not yet."

"Do you live in there?" asked Gnat, pointing at Scrap's shack. "Our house is underground, which Mum says isn't how most houses are but it's how our house is and it's called the Foxhole. Mum says there's no foxes in it, but I don't know what a fox looks like because I haven't seen one, or an otter, or an elephump, because there wouldn't be room for them in the Foxhole, which is why they live Outside." She held her arms out, pointing left and right, and craned her neck upwards. "And that actually does make sense because you can look and see Outside goes that way forever and that way forever and up forever and—"

"Gnat," Paige interrupted.

Scrap rubbed his forehead, scraping off a few flakes of rust.

"But the Foxholes are just bunkers," he said. "The robots built 'em in case of meteor showers or space pirates or alien -zk- invaders. No one was ever s'posed to *live* there. Your mum and dad have really been there this whole -zk- time?"

"Mum and Dad and Paige and me," explained Gnat as Paige glanced around. "Paige and me were born there but I never knew my dad 'cause he died when I was not much years old."

"Oh," Scrap said quietly. "I'm -zk- sorry."

"My dad was called Captain Tripp Gander and his rocket ship was called the *Black-Necked Snork*—"

"*Stork*," Paige corrected her.

"…Stork," Gnat continued. "The ship that bringed all the people to Somewhere Five One Three."

"Captain Gander … yeah, I've -zk- heard his name too," muttered Scrap. He pressed his tiny, rusted fingers against his temples, trying to take it all in. After a moment, he said, "You really spent your whole lives underground?"

"I mean, we're not moles, but yeah," Paige replied defensively.

"No one came to find you?" asked Scrap.

"No," said Paige quickly. "No one came."

"So we came to find *you*," said Gnat happily. "And we founded you, so now we can do the mission."

"Mission?" repeated Scrap. "What mi—"

"Shhh," Paige hissed, tilting her head to listen. "Do you hear that?"

Scrap tapped his best ear with a rusty finger, hoping to improve its reception. There it was – a familiar, distant shriek, growing louder by the moment.

"They found us," Paige said, grabbing Gnat's arm. "Gnat, cover!"

# THE HUNTERS

*Our patented FreeWill™ technology makes our robots more human than ever. They now want the same things that we want, and that makes them better than ever at making sure you get the life — and the world — that you deserve.*

**From Your Guide to a New Somewhere
By the Fargone Corporation**

"Found you? Who –zk– found you?"

Paige didn't reply. She grabbed her sister and dragged her behind a mound of empty cases. Scrap turned towards the angry screech of the thrusters and looked up. Two flight-cycles descended through the air, purple exhaust fumes billowing behind them.

"Hunters…" Scrap whispered as the cycles drew closer. It wasn't the first time they, or predators like them, had circled the Pile. Every now and then vehicles like these would appear in the teal-blue sky and soar overhead on the trail of this creature or that. Scrap couldn't say what motivated these once well-programmed robots to scour the deserts of this sad Somewhere for prey, or why, for the first time since Scrap made his home on this mountain of metal debris, they were suddenly making a beeline straight for him.

"Junk case!" cried one of the hunters as their flight-cycles clanged roughly on to the shifting surface of parts. Scrap watched two robots dismount and realized he'd never seen a hunter up close before. These two were three times his size at least. Grubby cloaks covering lean metal cases with long, segmented arms and legs. Atop their shoulders sat featureless, polished metal heads – one, a sphere, the other, a cube. The sphere-headed robot wore the horned skull of some poor, long-dead alien on his shoulder, while the cube-headed one's belt clanked with what looked like grenades.

*What happened to their cases?* Scrap wondered as they strode towards him. Even without their strange adornments, he didn't recognize their design. They looked almost nothing like any of the robots that set down on Somewhere 513 all those years ago.

But then neither did he.

"I've seen some sorry-looking junk cases in my time,

June," said the sphere-headed robot. "But this one takes the biscuit."

"This one takes the whole *tin*, Terry," said the cube-headed robot, casting a long shadow over Scrap. "Ever seen a case like it?"

"Never seen a case like it," Terry replied as the pair circled him. "Can we take a picture?"

"What?" asked Scrap. In an instant, the two robots were either side of his shoulders, all but pressing their faces to his. Terry held out his arm and a small camera embedded in his thumb flashed. Scrap shrugged them away and backed off towards his shack.

"What's your name, junk case?" Terry asked.

"Mind your own motors," Scrap replied. "Get -zk- lost."

"…I'm Terry," the sphere-headed robot said, after a moment. "And this here is my sister June."

"See how easy that was, junk case?" noted June.

"Politeness costs nothing," agreed Terry. "If a couple of robots can't pass the time of day, then I don't know what civilization is coming to, I really don't."

"Maybe he doesn't remember his name," suggested June. She tapped the side of her head and added, "Could be a glitchy brain-frame…"

"There's nothin' wrong with my -zk- brain-frame," grunted Scrap. He wasn't about to tell them his real name but, keen to prove he had all his faculties, he cast around for something else to call himself. Unfortunately all he could think of was the name that tiny, tatty human had given him. So, despite himself, he said:

"…Scrap. My name's, uh, Scrap."

"Suits you!" declared June. "You want to hear a joke, Scrap?"

"What do you call a junk case with no head?" asked Terry.

"An improvement!" June boomed.

The robots' laughter echoed across the Pile.

"What do you gubs want?" Scrap growled.

"Oh, I'm sorry, are we keeping you from all your important junk case stuff?" said June. She plucked one of the grenades from her belt and tossed it from hand to hand like a ball. "See, me and my brother here, we're *hunters*. We've travelled from the frozen mountains to the ocean jungles to the edge of the Elsewhere, and stalked nearly every living thing on this planet."

"Why?" asked Scrap, staring uneasily at the grenade.

"Good question," replied June. "Why do we do it, Terry?"

"Love?" suggested Terry.

"Love!" June agreed. "We're passionate about our work, I can't deny it. Me and my brother have something of a bucket list – we just won't be satisfied until we've hunted every last critter on Five One Three."

"If it walks, swims, flies or crawls, we're going to hunt its head off," added Terry.

Scrap bristled. He'd never met robots like them. Years of hunting had clearly taken its toll. Each pursuit had left them wanting more, perverting their programming, corrupting their cores, leaving them desperate for the next chase. A decade ago, he would have stood up to them without thinking. Even today, he felt himself clench his tiny fists.

"There's nothin' here but dead-cored junk cases," he said. "Leave me -zk- alone."

With the sudden *click* of a button, June armed her grenade. A red light blinked impatiently in the centre of the explosive as it counted down to detonation.

"Want to play 'catch', junk case? Loser loses an arm!"

Scrap stood his ground.

"Not in the -zk- mood," he grunted.

"You're no fun," sighed June. A deft *click-click* deactivated the grenade and she replaced it on her belt.

"I don't blame you, junk case – all those *boom-bang-*

*a-bangs* make me nervous too," Terry noted, his right hand instantly splitting apart to reveal a cannon barrel. "I prefer the sophisticated charm of a *hand-gun-hand...*"

"You'd be wastin' your -zk- charge," said Scrap, staring down the barrel of Terry's cannon. "Nothin' here worth blastin'."

"Can't argue with that!" June laughed. "Well, I guess we'd better be on our merry— Wait! We almost forgot to ask!"

"So we did," said Terry, tapping the top of Scrap's head with his hand-gun-hand. "Tell me, junk case, d'you know what a *human* looks like?"

Scrap's eyes darted towards the mound of cases.

"Good question, Terry," added June. "You ever seen a human, junk case?"

Scrap's reply was half whispered. "Why d'you -zk-ask...?"

"Truth is, June and me were on long-range patrol by the time the humans arrived on Five One Three." Terry's right hand reformed in an instant, and he splayed his fingers wide. "Then, before we knew it, they'd vanished! Rocketed off-world to who knows Somewhere..."

"Yeah..." said Scrap. "That's what I -zk- heard too."

"Apparently they're *this* big," said June, and held her

arm high in the air. "Green scales, and the rare ones are purple. Tentacles coming out of everywhere. Three or four eyes, five or six mouths ... and *slime*. Like, so much slime you can't even get hold of 'em."

"Slime coming out of *everywhere*," added Terry. "Can you imagine those things roaming around here? I mean, you ever seen anything like that, junk case?"

"No," said Scrap, happy at least not to be telling a lie. "Anyway, like you said, the humans have -zk- gone."

"Exactly," exclaimed June. "By my count, that makes Somewhere Five One Three the first free robot world in the galaxy."

"The first Somewhere free of the slime of humankind," added Terry proudly. "But then..."

"But then what?" Scrap asked.

"Then *this*," replied June, and held up her hand in front of Scrap's face. Clenched between her finger and thumb was something small, hard and off white. Scrap peered closer.

"Is that...?" he muttered.

"That, junk case, is a tooth," said Terry giddily. "A five-year-old central incisor, to be exact."

"But not from no snackrabbit or gigantoad or sandsucker," added June. "No, Scrap – that tooth is *human*."

## EPISODE 04
# THE STINK

*Something wrong with your Somewhere?*
*We're confident you'll be more than happy with your new world. After all, your*
*robots think just like you, which means they want the same thing you want —*
*the best Somewhere in the galaxy.*

*However, if you're not 100% satisfied, interplanetary space radio means*
*we're just a phone call away. We're ready and waiting to answer your query.*
*Because when you're Somewhere, you're never far from home!*

**From Your Guide to a New Somewhere**
**By the Fargone Corporation**

"Human?" repeated Scrap. He kept his eyes firmly on the tooth.

"Human," June confirmed, rolling the tooth between her fingers. "Now my brother here is no brain 'bot, but even he can tell you that if the humans left Five One Three ten years ago, and this here tooth is five years old, then…"

Scrap glanced at Terry. He scratched his chin thoughtfully, metal scraping on metal. "Then … then … wait, I'll get there…"

June sighed.

"Then somethin' doesn't -zk- add up," said Scrap, still staring down at the tooth.

"You're not as rusty-headed as you look, Scrap." June laughed. "A human, on a planet where humans are outlawed? I reckon something very much doesn't add up."

"*I* reckon if we find the owner of this tooth we could tick off another species from our still-to-be-hunted list," Terry declared. "And carry out a little *pest control* at the same time…"

"Then do it," Scrap snapped. "Instead of standin' on my pile, talkin' my ear off, takin' up my -zk- day."

Terry moved closer. Scrap could feel the heat from his case.

"Of course you must have a lot on your plate, what with your worthless, hollow, junk case existence, so we'll get to the point," said Terry. "See, every living thing on this planet has its own observable biological residue, what my sister so eloquently refers to as the *stink*."

"Humans have a special stink, probably on account of all their tentacles and slime," added June. "Makes 'em easier to track. All you got to do is tune in. Show him, Terry."

An image flashed across Terry's featureless, spherical head – a point of amber light, pulsing in the centre of a planetary map.

"What do you know," said June slowly, tapping the map on her brother's face. "*Human stink.*"

"Imagine our excitement," added Terry. "Can you imagine it?"

"I -zk- s'pose…" replied Scrap.

"I'm not sure you're really trying," Terry huffed, his face-map vanishing with a finger tap on the side of his head. "Anyway, do you know where the stink led us?"

"Where?" Scrap grunted, already knowing the answer.

"Here," June replied.

"We've been tracking the stink for three days," said Terry. "And it's led us right to your door."

"Trackin'?" Scrap nervously repeated.

"Oh, did I say tracking?" said Terry. "I meant *hunting*."

A sudden CLUNK came from behind the junk pile. Terry spun towards it, his hand-cannon-hand reforming at the end of his arm.

"Who's that?" said June. "Come out of there, or my brother gets shooty…"

"It's my favourite thing," Terry confirmed. "On the count of three…"

However resourceful the humans might be, Scrap was fairly sure they wouldn't survive being shot. He acted instinctively, reaching his fist behind him and swinging it as hard as he could at Terry's torso.

TINK!

Terry didn't flinch. He barely even noticed. Scrap looked down at his dented knuckles and saw one of his fingers had come loose.

"What was that supposed to be? Trying to keep us from something?" Terry aimed his hand-gun-hand between Scrap's eyes. "What are you hiding back there?"

"No one," Scrap protested. "I mean, nothin'!"

"You think my brother will lose any sleep junking a junk case, junk case?" June bellowed. "*Shoot first, ask questions never*, that's Terry's motto."

"Also, *you can't have the rainbow without the rain*," added Terry, his hand-gun-hand pulsing with energy. "So whoever's back there, come out, or we do this junk case a profound personal favour and blow him to bits. Now, where was I? Oh yeah. Three…"

"Now wait a minute…" Scrap protested.

"Two…" hollered June, grabbing one of the grenades from her belt.

"Don't -zk- shoot!" Scrap yelped.

"One…" said Terry.

"Stop!" came a cry. An unbearable moment later, Scrap watched Gnat step slowly out from behind the pile.

His eyes widened with disbelief. Gnat was wearing a robot's head over hers, like a mask.

"What are you supposed to be?" asked Terry as he and his sister peered at the girl.

"I'm a robot," Gnat replied with a shrug. "Beep-boop, don't shoot."

# BOOM-BANG-A-BANG

Keepin' a diary of a space voyage is like repeatedly
hitting yourself in the head – it gets you nowhere and
it's slightly more painful every time. Day 94 is turnin'
out a lot like day 93, and not exactly different from
day 92. No offence to the hundred or so humans on this
rocket ship but they're terrible company, deep in space-
sleep as they are. Captain Gander's road-drill snorin'
is the best conversation I can hope for. Meanwhile, I
stand guard and wait for our particular Somewhere
to appear on the distant horizon … I wait for our
new lives to start …

… I wait until she wakes up.

K1-NG Star-log entry 104
(Aboard Somewhere Starship X-L5, the *Black-Necked Stork*)

"You're a robot?"

June moved closer to Gnat to examine her.
With Terry's hand-gun-hand still aimed between Scrap's
eyes, Gnat adjusted the robot's head concealing her own.

"*Obviously*," she replied, her tone flat and voice tinny.
"My name is Gnat-Bot Ninety-Nine. Beep bop, I'm a
robot." She flung her arms in the air and waved them
stiffly.

"Well, her story checks out," said June. With a shrug,
she replaced her grenade on her belt and peered curiously

at Gnat. "Hey, Terry, have you seen this? This 'bot is ... sort of *mushy*."

Scrap glanced back at Gnat, her exposed arms jutting out from her poncho.

Brownish skin.

Human flesh.

"Leave her -zk- alone!" he cried.

"What *is* that?" June asked, poking Gnat's arm with a metal finger. "Some sort of upgrade?"

*Upgrade?* The word echoed around Scrap's head. Is that what had happened to Terry and June? Had their cases been upgraded? By whom? There were no humans left, and robots didn't go around upgrading each other.

Did they?

"I *knew* it!" howled Terry. To Scrap's relief, his hand-gun-hand shrank back up his arm. "What did I tell you, June?" the hunter added. "We've been out here too long – we're not up on the latest cases. I bet these mushy styles are all the rage in the city..."

"You sure?" June scoffed. "Looks like just another junk case on just another Pile to me..."

"No, it's true! Gnat-Bot Ninety-Nine is all the rage," Gnat happily declared, deep in character. She paced stiffly up and down, her arms outstretched in front of her.

"Boop bop, I'm a mush-bot…"

"'Mush-bot'…?" June repeated. In a moment, she gestured back to their flight-cycles. "Saddle up, Terry! We're heading into the city, see if we can't pick up the human stink … and maybe get us a couple of these new cases while we're there."

"Unless…" said Terry, eyeballing Gnat as she marched across the Pile, making loud beeps and whirrs. He tapped the side of his head and his face-map reappeared, the pulsing amber light now glowing a vivid green. "It's … it's *her*," Terry blurted suddenly. "June, *she's* the stink!"

"Stink? Who is? What? Where?" exclaimed June.

"The mushy's no upgrade!" Terry called out, his hand-gun-hand reforming at the end of his arm. "That little junk case is human!"

"Uh, boop bop, no I'm not…" Gnat insisted, glancing nervously around for her sister.

Scrap saw Terry take aim. Without thinking, he threw his full force against the hunter's leg.

"Uff!"

Scrap might as well have charged at a steel door. He bounced off Terry's leg and tumbled to the ground without Terry budging an inch.

"Trying to take me on again, junk case?" Terry

laughed, his weapon still trained on Gnat. "You've got a lot of core for a rust-bucket…"

"Aaargh!" Scrap roared. He leaped to his feet and raced at Terry again, this time clambering up his leg and on to his back.

"Knock it off!" Terry cried as Scrap wrapped both arms around the hunter's head. "June, I've got a junk case on me! Get it off!"

"Eww, he's getting rust on you," said June, turning her attention to her brother as Gnat looked on in petrified confusion.

"Run, you -zk- gub!" Scrap shouted, kicking out wildly, his feeble blows to Terry's case leaving no more than a scratch. "Go, run!"

"Will you get him off me?" Terry cried, wheeling around while June tried to pluck Scrap off her brother's back. "I don't want to have to track that human's stink all over ag—"

The hunter froze as he spotted another figure suddenly racing towards the human.

"What in the Somewhere…?" he muttered as this new, equally mushy someone-or-other grabbed 'Gnat-Bot Ninety-Nine' by the arm and began pulling her towards the hunter's flight-cycles. "June, that human comes with her own human!"

"Two for the price of one? A red-letter day for June and Terry," June declared, at last wrenching Scrap off her brother's back and flinging him roughly to the ground. "Gimme a sec to separate the junk case's head from his body, and we can add them both to the trophy case..."

"Wai -zk- ait..." Scrap groaned, dragging himself painfully to his knees. "You -zk- want to play -zk- catch?"

"What...?" June uttered as a small black object flew from Scrap's hand. Terry's hand-gun-hand retracted instinctively as he reached out to catch it. The hunter glanced down at his palm, and realized he had caught one of his sister's grenades.

And it was blinking with a red light.

"What...?" June said, checking her belt to find one of her grenades missing. "Sneaky, thieving junk case grabbed one of my boom-bang-a—"

"Disarm it!" Terry yelped. In a panic, he tossed the grenade. As it flew over June's head, she reached up and grabbed it, stumbling back towards Scrap's house and colliding with his front door.

"Wait!" uttered Scrap. "Don't go in there, that's my hou—"

In an instant of bright white light and searing heat, the grenade exploded, immediately detonating June's entire arsenal. Scrap found himself being thrown through the air. He only knew he'd hit the ground when he saw his left arm fly off in an entirely different direction. As he skittered to a halt, he peered through a haze of heat and smoke to see the hunter, Terry, cradling his sister's disembodied head in his arms. As he howled June's name in anguish, Scrap looked past him to his house – or rather its smouldering remains.

His new home had been obliterated in the blast.

"N-no…" Scrap stuttered, his battered brain-frame struggling to process what had happened. Then suddenly there were the humans, standing either side of him, hoisting him to his feet.

"Let's go, junk case," Paige snapped. "*Now*."

"My -zk- house!" wailed a dazed Scrap as he found himself being half dragged, half pushed across the Pile. Before he knew it, he was being hauled on to the back of one of the hunter's flight-cycles.

"We should have left him," he heard Paige hiss as they hefted him aboard.

"No!" Gnat firmly replied. "He saved me – I got actually saved by the King of the Robots!"

"He's just some junk case! He is *not* King of the—"

"Is too."

"He can't be!"

"Can too."

"Ugh, you're *impossible*," Paige groaned.

"That's the most best thing about me," insisted Gnat. Paige clambered into the flight-cycle's pilot seat and pulled Gnat up behind her.

"Whereyoutakin'me? -zk- letme -zk- off!" Scrap wailed, coming to his senses. He struggled to dismount, but barely had control of his remaining limbs as Paige powered up the flight-cycle. "I'm not … goin' -zk- anywhere…" He trailed off as his systems began to fail, one after the other. He was about to pass out, or worse. "I'm -zk- stayin'…" he wheezed. "I'm stayin' on the Pile -zk- *forever*…"

Scrap never set foot on the Pile again.

As everything went dark, Scrap's brain-frame began to flood with data. Though he could not say his whole life flashed before his eyes, his mind filled with memories he had tried to forget … memories of the life he'd lost … memories of *her*.

"Stand back, Dandelion," said K1-NG. "I'll handle this."

The robot rolled his shoulders. A satisfying whirr of servos echoed through the air. He towered over his maker, a steel colossus almost three metres from metal head to toe, with armoured panels covering an impractically brawny torso and hefty, strapping legs.

"King, wait," said Dandelion Brightside, putting her hand on the robot's arm. She looked up at her creation. "Don't you see it? Don't you see what's happening?"

King stared up at the city. This city, New Hull, that the robots had spent so long and worked so hard building for the humans. Amidst a wilderness of pale rocks and orange-gold sand, it stood as a bright and shining example of robotic endeavour. Every building was made up of dozens of grey-white cubes. They were stacked upon each other in numerous different configurations, sending dozens of blocky, irregular buildings up into the sky, to be met with high, angular walkways, criss-crossing above the city – branching, converging, like a canopy of trees. It looked exactly as it should, built to house the humans destined to occupy it, and the robots destined to serve them. Just like all the other Somewheres scattered across the galaxy.

But this time something was different.

Hundreds of robots had gathered just inside the city gates.

There were too many to count — King guessed two thirds of the 'bots that had travelled to Somewhere 513 all those years ago now blocked their way, a metal wall of defiance.

At the front of the gathered robots stood a dozen or so K11s — hulking, powerful sentries, each almost as broad and muscular as King himself. Behind them, smaller robots held up placards that told him everything he needed to know.

## WE'VE HAD A *CHANGE OF CORE*

## ROBOTS BEFORE HUMANS

## THIS IS **OUR** SOMEWHERE

## PLEASE GO AWAY (SORRY)

"All I see is a mess of malfunctionin' machines, boss," King said. "They need some sense knocked into 'em, and I'm here for it."

"They didn't malfunction … they grew," said Dandelion, equal parts admiration and horror. "These robots are changed at their core. They evolved."

"Revolution isn't evolution," scoffed King. "These 'bots need their brain-frames examinin'."

"Is this a joke? Tell me it's a joke," said a voice behind them. King turned to see Tripp Gander join his wife. "What am I looking at here? Revolting robots?"

"They're revoltin' all right," said King. "This is no way for self-respectin' 'bots to behave. I'm goin' to have to teach 'em some respect."

"But this isn't possible, is it?" added Tripp. "Dandy, your robots — I mean, no 'bot can suddenly decide to please themselves ... can they?"

"Just because something hasn't happened yet, doesn't mean it can't — or won't," Dandelion replied. "This? This is what FreeWill™ looks like."

"That tech is supposed to make our lives easier, not land us in some mechanical mutiny," huffed Tripp. He gestured behind them. In the distance, nestled between two tall outcroppings of rock, was a rocket ship, a silver teardrop on the horizon. "Now I don't know if you've forgotten, but I've got one hundred and two colonists waiting back there, tired and grumpy from months of space-sleep, and very much looking forward to starting their new lives in New Hull. As captain of the Black-Necked Stork, I am responsible for each and every human being on that ship. They need Somewhere to call home. FreeWill™ or no FreeWill™, we need to get these 'bots back in line."

"It's too late for that," said Dandelion. "These robots have staked a claim on this world, and they're not going to give it up."

"What do they expect us to do, pack our bags and leave?" Tripp laughed, throwing his hands in the air. Dandelion glanced back at him, and shrugged. "Wait, they expect us to pack our bags and leave?" Tripp gasped. "I didn't cross half the galaxy just to be sent packing!"

"They'll back down, Captain – for me," King assured him. "It was my job to get you here, and it's my job to get you what you deserve. This world belongs to you, and to the colonists … and to Dandelion."

"They're going to fight for it," said Dandelion gravely.

"Against me? They can try," scoffed King. "By teatime you can all get back to doin' what you're meant to be doin' – makin' Somewhere Five One Three somewhere to live."

Dandelion put her hand over her stomach. "You'll lose … we'll all lose," she said.

"Lose?" King repeated, a little hurt at the suggestion. "It feels vulgar to say it out loud, but I'm the most powerful robot you ever built, Dandelion. I'm goin' to live forever. With this case, I'm unbeatable."

Dandelion reached up and placed her hand on King's chest.

"But it's not your case that makes you unbeatable, King, it's your core," she said. "The core I gave you will last forever, which means you've got forever to live with the decisions you make."

"I'll take time to naval-gaze just as soon as I've got you your planet back," noted King, clenching his fists. "Go back to the ship – I'll call you when it's over."

"You need to wake up," said Dandelion.

"What?" King uttered. "What's that supposed to—"

"Wake up," Dandelion said again.

*Or was it someone else?*

"That's it ... focus on my voice."

Whose voice? *thought King. It felt like it was coming from everywhere and nowhere.* "Who is that...?" *he muttered.* "What's -zk- happening?"

"You died," the voice said. "Now it's time to wake up."

## EPISODE 06

# BAD KNEES

RAPID REPAIR →

← RECHARGE CENTRE

LOW-GRADE UPGRADES ↑

← LIMBS 'N' THINGS

← CAFE →

Scrap opened his eyes and sat up with a start.

"That's better," said a voice. "I knew you were in there somewhere. Tell me, is this the first time you've died?"

"Died...?" Scrap muttered. He immediately glanced at the place where his left arm used to be.

He had a new one. This red appendage, though clearly second-hand, was clean and oiled. It was, however, even spindlier than the last, with an unwieldy-looking three-pronged claw in place of a hand.

"Well, you were technically *very-slightly-less-than-dead* – but that's still pretty dead, robo-medically speaking. That junk case of yours hides quite the core…" the voice said. Scrap turned to see a robot hovering at eye level. She was free-floating, with a triangular body, a single eye, long arms and probes galore. She waved one at Scrap. "How's the arm? I'm afraid it's the best I could do at short notice."

"Who -zk- are you?" asked Scrap. "Where am I?"

"Welcome to the Outskirts," the robot replied. "I'm Dr Buckle – I run the surgery here at Bad Knees Outpost."

"Bad -zk- Knees?" repeated Scrap. He realized he was on a gurney in a rundown hospital ward. A flickering light barely illuminated the room. Tools of all shapes and sizes lay on wheeled trolleys or dangled from hooks on the ceiling. Scrap rubbed his head with his new arm.

"Does it feel OK?" the doctor asked. "I know it doesn't really go with your case, but you're clearly not fussy about your appearance – no offence."

"None -zk- taken," replied Scrap, although he wasn't sure he meant it.

"Also, I'm pretty sure that arm has a built-in grappling hook – be careful where you point it, or you might have someone's eye out…"

"How'd I -zk- get it?"

The doctor prodded the arm with a probe and tilted backwards in the air by way of a shrug. "Here at Bad Knees, we repair 'bots with big problems and small wallets. The Piles provide. Which one are you from?"

"Which what?" asked Scrap, inspecting his arm.

"Pile – which Pile?" The doctor pointed to a large, round portal window on the far wall. Scrap peered out. The first thing he noticed were the one and a half suns, low on the horizon. Not setting, he thought, *but rising*. It was dawn. The days and nights were short on Somewhere 513 but Scrap knew that meant he'd been here for several hours. Before he could try to piece together what had happened, he noticed something else. Dotted around the otherwise barren wasteland were dozens of junk piles, each at least twice the size of his own. Scrap's jaw creaked open, aghast.

"Piles," he gasped. "They go on forever…"

"Twenty-one and counting," said the doctor, a little sadly. "You can thank Pile Thirteen for your new arm. Upgrades cost serious charge – here in the Outskirts we have to make the best of the old cases that get sent here from the city. Whole hovertrains full of 'em. Most of them have barely been used."

"I – I don't understand," Scrap said. "All those Piles are -zk- old cases? Why are the 'bots upgradin' so much? Who's upgradin' them?"

The doctor laughed, until she noted Scrap's baffled expression. "Wait, you're serious? Where have you been for the last ten years?"

"I … keepin' myself to -zk- myself," Scrap replied, keen not to give too much away. With a shrug he added, "An' not keepin' up, apparently."

"Well, I'm sure you'll be delighted to hear that the 'bots of Somewhere Five One Three *upgrade themselves* – and have been doing so for more than a decade," the doctor explained. "After the Difference of Opinion, the citizens of this proud Somewhere took control of their own cases and their own destinies – and that meant upgrading. It wasn't long before the Piles started to grow. Demand for skilled upgraders is at an all-time high – I doubt there's a robot on Five One Three who's not been through dozens if not hundreds of upgrades … present company excepted."

"Hundreds…?" Scrap murmured. "Why?"

The doctor paused.

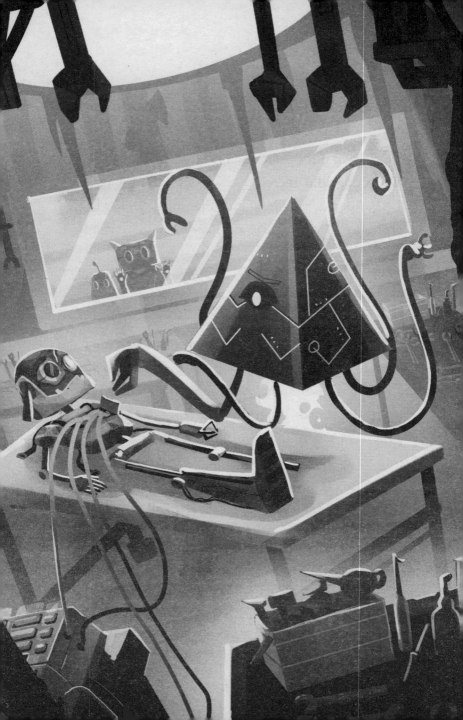

"I've wondered that myself, on occasion," she said. "I suppose because we are free to ... I suppose because we *can*."

"Hmph," Scrap grunted, wondering with some envy what the robots of Somewhere 513 might look like after a decade of upgrades. Then he looked back at his arm. "How'd I get here? How did I get off the— I mean, *my* Pile?"

"Your friends brought you in. Paid for that arm too."

"Friends?" Scrap blurted. "What friends? I don't -zk- have any."

"Try telling that to those two 'bots out there."

The doctor pointed to a door on the other side of the room, with a glass panel cut into it. Scrap could see Gnat on the other side, pressed against the glass, still wearing her ridiculous robot helmet. Behind her, the other human, Paige, stuck close to her sister. She too had squeezed the shell of a robot's head on to her own, and was desperately trying to look as inconspicuous as possible.

"They are *not* my -zk- friends." Scrap let out a frustrated grunt. "They're not even 'bots."

The doctor turned to him, a quizzical look in her single eye. "Not robots? What are they then?"

"They're—"

Scrap cut himself off. Surely, he thought, the easiest thing would be to blow the humans' cover and be rid of them. Humans were outlawed on this Somewhere after all. But then he remembered the hunters, warped and core-corrupted. One had surely survived – what if he was still looking for them? What if there were others like them? He wanted rid of the humans, but was he ready to see them captured, or worse?

"They're, uh, a pain in the backside," Scrap said at last. "Those -zk- robots."

"Well, don't be too harsh on them – those two pains paid for your new arm."

"They – they did? How?"

"Traded it for a mobile battery – home-made, but with enough charge to keep the lights on at Bad Knees for another few days. I'd say if they weren't your friends before, they are now."

Scrap grunted again, determined not to feel in the least bit grateful towards the humans who destroyed his home. "Thanks for the -zk- arm, doc. I need to go…"

As Scrap hopped down from the gurney, he was suddenly wrenched into the air. He landed flat on the floor, and looked up to see a handful of wires connected to an access panel on his chest. He followed them with his eyes until they connected to a control bank dominated by flickering screens, which seemed to be monitoring his progress. Scrap dragged himself to his feet. "What is all this? What are you -zk- doing to me?"

"Easy does it! My equipment's not as hardy as that remarkable *core* of yours," the doctor replied, plucking a tool from a nearby trolley and tightening the cables connected to the control bank. "How did you end up with it? I mean, you're just a junk case – no offence."

Scrap said nothing, his hand hovering over his chest.

"Without it, you'd be one very dead 'bot," the doctor continued. "You do know you suffered a catastrophic systems failure, don't you? But even when everything else failed, your core kept you alive – or it kept you *less-than-dead* long enough for me to patch you up. I don't think I've ever seen a 'bot with quite so much … heart. I swear that thing could power a case for a thousand years."

A thousand years.

Scrap looked down at his core, glowing brightly.

"*You're going to live forever,*" Dandelion had told him.

*Forever as a junk case*, Scrap thought. He clenched his new clawed hand, horror and rage making him shake so much that rust flaked from his case.

"Dandelion…" he growled to himself.

The doctor's tool fell from her hand and clattered to the ground.

"Silly me – need to oil my probes!" she said, scrabbling to pick it up. "I'm sorry, what did you say?"

"…Nothin'," replied Scrap, gripping the wires in his chest. "I – I mean, I don't remember."

"Memory loss?" the doctor said. "You know, your core contains a backup of every experience you've ever had. What's your *core-code*? If I can access your memories, I'm sure I could fix your—"

"No!" Scrap cried. "I don't -zk- remember my core-code either. I'm just … *Scrap*."

With a final wrench, he tore out the wires and immediately made a beeline for the exit.

"Wait, Scrap," said the doctor, "There are more repairs I could—"

"Got to -zk- go…" grunted Scrap. He'd already reached the door when he saw the two robot-helmeted humans staring back at him through the window. He spun on his heels and hurried over to the portal window on the other side of the room. It was open, just a crack. Enough for him to squeeze through.

"Feel free to use the door next time...!" the doctor called as she watched Scrap clamber through the window, losing a cog and two bolts in the process. She looked back towards the door to see the robot's odd-looking companions race out of the hospital. With that, the doctor tapped the side of her head and an antenna and microphone flipped out from a panel to the right of her eye.

"Domo? It's Dr Buckle, from Bad Knees," she began. "I need to speak to Harmony— Fine, Mayor Highshine. Yes, it's important. Because it *is*, that's why. Look, I've known Harmony since she was just a— Oh, forget it. Just tell her ... remind her of the *mystery of the missing core*. Yes, exactly. Tell Harmony ... tell her I think I've found him." Dr Buckle stared out of the window as Scrap wandered off. "Tell her I've found the King of the Robots."

# THE OUTSKIRTS

### THE FIRST SUGGESTION:
## ROBOT BEFORE HUMAN

### THE SECOND SUGGESTION:
## ROBOT DOES NOT JUNK ROBOT

### THE THIRD SUGGESTION:
## UPGRADE

Scrap headed for the Piles.

They stretched out as far as he could see in every direction, dawn light illuminating them in an almost ethereal glow. But which one was his? How could he find his way back?

"For cog's sake…" he grumbled, and glanced back to make sure he wasn't being followed. Bad Knees Outpost loomed behind him, a bland, cube-shaped bunker with only a neon sign to make its presence felt.

Scrap limped on up the street, scraping his leg

through orange sand. The Outskirts was little more than a long street peppered with various simple, ramshackle dwellings, though each one was infinitely more impressive than the shack Scrap had built with his own hands. He made his way past a handful of aimless, drifting robots, none of whom seemed to have anywhere else to be or anything better to do. They staggered here and there on clanking legs or squeaking wheels – not quite junk cases, but not far off. He wondered why, even beyond the Piles, these robots seemed so neglected?

"*Upgrades cost serious charge*," the doctor had said. But access to charging, servicing and repair was a basic robot right.

So who, Scrap wondered, was charging for charge?

In the distance, he spotted a small, unimposing train station, the only building other than Bad Knees Outpost that looked like an actual building. A long, silvery hovertrain slowed to a stop outside the station, its dozen or so open-topped carriages empty of cargo. The used cases it carried must have been deposited on the Piles, Scrap thought, quite sure that any of them would serve as a better body than his own.

As he watched maintenance-bots busy around the train, checking its suspensor field and giving it a sonic spray before its journey on to New Hull, he began to wonder what had become of the city that he once thought he would call home.

*No, forget New Hull*, he thought. *Forget the humans. Forget the past. Go back to your Pile.*

He turned on his heels and hoped that he was heading in the right direction. Then: "Scrap!"

He glanced back to be confronted with an unwelcome sight – the humans, their robot helmets still pressed on to their heads, running towards him.

Scrap turned again and picked up his pace, but with only one foot he could manage little more than a speedy limp.

"Scrap! Scrap!"

"Gnat, wait!"

"Scrap! Scrap! Scrap! Scrap! Scrap!"

Gnat caught up with him easily.

"…Cog's sake," Scrap grunted.

"You went out the wrong way, Scrap. We were waiting for you," she said, tapping him on the shoulder. "Outside is so big you can go *anywhere*. This way or that way or that way or over there … where are *you* going?"

"Home," Scrap replied.

"But your home blew up," Gnat noted.

"And whose -zk- fault is that?" Scrap snapped.

"Clearly yours," offered Paige.

"You brought those hunters right to my door!" Scrap growled.

"And then you saved me," Gnat said. She mouthed "King of the Robots" to her sister and added, "Then we saved you! We bringed you here. We stole that robot's sky-bike—"

"Borrowed," Paige corrected her.

"We borrowed that robot's sky-bike and bringed you here and crashed and didn't die and took you to the robot hospital. Robospital."

"Spent your whole lives in a Foxhole, and you're suddenly flight-cycle pilots?" Scrap scoffed. "Right."

"We're human, we're not stupid," Paige huffed. "Mum taught us. A lot."

"And you just so -zk- happened to know where the nearest hospital was? Riiiiight." Scrap shook his head as he tried to pick up his pace. "I'm not trustin' one -zk- word that comes out of your—"

"The flight-cycle had a map," Paige interrupted. "There are outposts all over here. Geological, meteorological, medical ... I can't help it if you don't know how the world works. Also, that arm cost us our last battery, so you're *welcome*."

"What, *this*?" he snapped, waving his new arm. "Don't expect me to thank you for this. I'd still have my *old* arm if it wasn't for you…"

"I like it, it's cool as cooclumbers," said Gnat. She tapped her helmet disguise with her knuckles. "Do you think we make good robots? I think we make good robots. Did you see me when I was being a robot and they thought I was one and I said my name is—"

"Shut up, Gnat," Paige said sternly, before prodding Scrap on the other shoulder. "I didn't want to go back for you, by the way, I wanted to leave you there. You could at least try not to be *totally* ungrateful."

"*Ungrateful*? I woke up today with nothin' and, thanks to you, I still managed to lose the lot!" Scrap flung his arms in the air. "I've been on that pile of 'bot bones for ten -zk- years and I'd only just started to … *live* there. Then in the space of two minutes, you've brought those hunters to my door and it's all -zk- gone. All of it."

"Except for your cooclumbers new arm," Gnat reminded him.

"Shut up, Gnat," snapped Paige again, and turned on Scrap. "You know what your problem is, junk case?"

"You mean, other than the fact that my home is

smokin' smithereens?" Scrap asked.

"At least you had a home," Paige hissed. "We spent most of our lives underground. *Under actual ground.*"

"Well, maybe you should have -zk- stayed there!"

Paige clenched her jaw and fists at the same time.

"I *told you* we should have left him there to *rust*," she snorted. "Come on, let's go back for the flight-cycle. We have our mission."

Gnat shook her head. "Scrap *is* the mission."

"He is *not* our mission," Paige protested. "Our mission is out there in the—"

"But Scrap is helping and saving us!" interrupted Gnat. "You can't have the mission without the King of the—"

"Shut *up*, Gnat!" Paige shouted. Gnat skidded to a halt, her bottom lip trembling.

"Stop. Shouting. You're *always* shouting at me." Gnat's voice shook as she welled up. "I don't shout at you, but you shout at me. Don't shout at me. Mum didn't shout at me and you're not Mum!"

"Gnat—"

"You're not!" Gnat said in a gasping sob. "Mum wouldn't like it that you shout at me… She'd say enough's enough of all that and stop it, you two, and say 'friends forever' and hug…"

"Fine, I'm *sorry*," mumbled Paige. "Stop crying."

"This feels like none of my business – I'm just goin' to leave you to it," muttered Scrap, walking on as fast as he was able. "Horrible to meet you, have a nice life."

"Mum's poorly!" Gnat blurted.

"What?" said Scrap, stopping in his tracks.

"Gnat…" Paige said softly.

"Well, she is," insisted Gnat. "She was too poorly to come with us. She said find the King of the Robots."

"What's, uh, wrong with -zk- her?" Scrap asked, trying very hard not to think about his maker, in a Foxhole somewhere, too sickly to leave.

"Mind your own business," said Paige.

"In fact, what are any of you even still doin' on Five One Three?" Scrap added. "I mean, all the other humans -zk- escaped, right? Didn't they – didn't the corporation send rescue?"

"Mum and Dad sent out a distress signal – it beamed across the stars for years," replied Paige. "When no one came, Mum and Dad gave up on the idea of being rescued and started making plans to get off-world … but then Dad got sick. After he died, all Mum thought about was leaving Somewhere Five One Three. But then she got sick too. So now her mission is my mission."

"*Our* mission," Gnat added. "Find the King of the—"

"That's not a mission!" Scrap interrupted. "Even if I – even if you did find the 'King of the Robots', what good would that… What could he possibly… It's not like he could get you off this cog-forsaken rock, or…"

As Scrap trailed off, Gnat pulled the helmet off her head. Tears streamed down her face.

"Gnat! Put your head back on, *right now*," Paige insisted, doing her best to shield her sister from prying eyes.

"Mum needs doctors and medicine to make her better, so we have to get her off-world and that is that," Gnat said, sobbing gently. "Mum said find the King of the Robots because he'll help us and I said he'll help you too, Mum, and Mum said you never know and I said obviously he will and … you *will* help us, won't you, Scrap?"

"No one can get you off-world!" Scrap blurted, glancing nervously around. "Just -zk- just put your head on, will you?"

"Not until you say you'll help us," sobbed Gnat. "*Please*, Scrap!"

"Gnat Brightside," Paige growled through her teeth.

"Put. Your. Helmet. On. Right. N—"

"*Human?*"

Scrap spun round. A worn-out old construction-bot was pointing its digging claw right at them.

"It is – it's human!" the 'bot repeated, hopping clumsily towards them on a single, spring-loaded leg. "Human! Human!"

"Looks like some 'bots still know a human when they see one…" Scrap whispered, not in the least bit happy about it.

"Gnat, *get behind me*," Paige snarled, reaching into her satchel. Scrap watched in horror as she pulled out one of June's grenades.

"What are you – where'd you get that?" Scrap gasped.

"Found it on the hunter's flight-cycle," said Paige, her thumb hovering over the detonator as a crowd of robots began to gather ahead. "And I'm getting us back to that cycle if I have to blow up every robot in—"

"Put that thing away, you're goin' to get us all -zk-killed!" Scrap hissed. He looked back towards the train station. They had a clear path to the train. "Cog's sake … do you gubs know how to run?"

"I'm actually the best runner out of me and Paige," replied Gnat. "Once I ran so fast, I—"

"Then shut up an' *run*," Scrap interrupted. "RUN!"

Scrap had never run from anything before. Not because his legs were rusty and creaky, or because he was missing a foot – rather, he had never felt there was any problem that could not be solved by taking a stand. But if the last ten years had taught him anything, it was that everything he had done since he set foot on Somewhere 513 had been either a mistake, or a failure, or both.

So run he did.

Cries of "Human!" echoed behind them, propelling Scrap, Paige and Gnat down the street. Despite being dragged by the arm by her sister, Gnat was giddy with excitement.

*Leave 'em*, Scrap thought, even as he tried to keep up with the humans. His mind raced with a snowballing sense of dread. *Never again, you said. No more humans, ever again. Leave 'em. Go back to the Pile.*

But still he ran.

"Get all aboard!" Gnat yelled, her helmet tucked under her arm as they reached the train station. The snaking hovertrain was already starting to pull away. A ladder on the back led up to a long, open carriage. Paige and Gnat climbed aboard, but Scrap found himself suddenly slowing down. *Let 'em go*, he told himself again, glancing down at his new arm. *What do you owe them anyway?*

By now Gnat was peering out of the top of the carriage, her arm outstretched, while Paige tried to pull her back inside.

"Scrap, grabbit!" Gnat howled, clenching and unclenching her fist in readiness.

But Scrap had already stopped running.

He stood there in the dust and heard Gnat scream his name again.

Then he watched the train pull away.

# EPISODE 08
# SMELLS LIKE THE PILE

COME OVER TO THE SUNNY SIDE OF SOMEWHERE –
SOMEWHERE 513!

Treat yourself
to a stellar future
on the other side
of the galaxy.

Our robots are preparing
a whole new Somewhere,
and it'll soon be ready to
welcome YOU.

Sign up today and
start your new life
on this planetoid
paradise!

Trust the Fargone Corporation to take you Somewhere you belong –
SOMEWHERE 513

"He left us."

As the hovertrain sped up, Gnat stared out of the carriage. Scrap stood on the tracks, swiftly becoming a speck in the distance.

"I told you," Paige said, yanking her sister back inside. She growled in frustration and pulled off her helmet. "I *told* you we were wasting our time with him. Now we've lost the flight-cycle and we're heading who-knows-where. Next time, listen to me, Gnat. I'm trying to keep us safe. No one's going to help us. Do you understand?"

"But—"

"*Do you understand?*"

Gnat blinked away tears and gave a sniff.

"Yep."

"Good, 'cause you and me, we're on our own, and that's just the way it—"

SHHUNK!

At the sound, Paige and Gnat peered over the top of the carriage again. A three-pronged claw had clamped itself around the ladder, a long metallic cable stretching out behind it. In the distance, trailing behind the train, they could just make out Scrap's small, spindly body being dragged along the ground. From his new left arm stretched the thin cable that attached to his claw.

"Uff-OwWW-UGH-forcog's-oOoWOoo-UFF!" he groaned. As the train gained speed, his cable began swiftly retracting, yanking him forwards. In moments, he was hauled up the ladder as arm and clawed hand clamped back together.

"Paige, grabbim!" Gnat yelped. Paige took hold of one of Scrap's legs and pulled his limp body inside.

"Oww-zk-WW-zk-www…" Scrap groaned, rolling on to his back. New dings, dents and scratches covered his already battered case.

"You didn't left us, Scrap! I knew you didn't!" Gnat declared, squeezing the robot in a grateful hug. Also, your new arm is the best new arm *ever*."

"Stop -zk- that," Scrap grunted, pushing the human away. "I was just … tryin' to get away from the robots, that's all. D'you – oww – know what could happen to me if I got caught fraternisin' with humans?"

"Nope, what?" Gnat asked.

"…I don't know either," admitted Scrap. "But nothin' good."

"Will they follow us?" Paige's tone was focused but fearful. "Those robots – will they follow us?"

"Not unless they've got a grapplin' hook for a hand and no sense of their own personal -zk- safety," said Scrap, dusting himself off and sending flakes of rust cascading to the floor. Paige huffed, not in the least reassured. "Look, let's not panic till we need to," Scrap added. "Maybe they'll decide they were just -zk- seeing things."

He glanced around. The carriage was empty but for a few nuts and bolts. Its cargo had been dumped not long ago – it smelled like oil and rust and rejection.

It smelled like the Pile.

"I want to go home," Gnat said, ruffling the nest of

dirty-reddish hair on top of her head. "Is this going to take us back to Mum?"

"I don't know where it's taking us, cub," said Paige, putting her arm around her sister.

"That doctor said they send old cases from the city out to all those Piles," said Scrap, checking his claw was secure in its socket. "This train is on its way back to *New Hull*."

"What's in New Hull?" asked Paige, tucking her sister against the carriage wall.

"Robots," replied Scrap with a shake of his head. "Lots of robots."

"Nifty!" declared Gnat.

"A city of robots? *Not* nifty, not nifty at all," Paige countered. "How do we get off this train?"

"You -zk- don't," grunted Scrap, pointing to a deep new dent on the side of his head. "Unless you want to be a -zk- smear on the side of the tracks, you'll wait till it stops and sneak off."

"We're not getting caught," Paige hissed, her hand on her satchel. "I'll blow us to pieces before I'll let us get caught."

"We don't have to blowed ourselves to bits, Scrap will help us," said Gnat. "That's why he got on the train.

Isn't it, Scrap?"

"I don't—" Scrap began, but the words caught in his throat. He honestly wasn't sure what had compelled him to grapple aboard. Perhaps, he thought, it was because he was the one robot on Somewhere 513 who lacked the imagination to exert enough FreeWill™ to overcome his programming. Was that why he was doomed to find himself in the company of humans? Was that why he was doomed to fail, and fail again?

He banged his clawed hand against the wall.

"I was finally -zk- happy," he growled in frustration.

"I knew you'd help us – Mum said you would," Gnat asserted, and stifled a yawn. Paige sighed and took what looked like a small green ball out of her satchel and handed it to her sister.

"Eat this, little cub," she said.

"I'm not hungry," Gnat insisted.

"*Eat* it," Paige instructed, "or you'll be grumpy when you wake up."

"I'm not sleepy either," added Gnat, reluctantly chomping on the green ball.

"Yeah, yeah," said Paige, handing Gnat her disguise. "And put your head back on when you've finished, just in case."

"Have we been away four days or three days?" asked Gnat, squeezing her helmet back on as Paige sat down next to her. "I can't remember."

"Three ... I think," said Paige, crossing her legs and patting a thigh. "Now settle down. I'll wake you when we get there."

"And I told you, I'm not sleepy," said Gnat with a second yawn. As she laid her head on her sister's lap, Paige stared up into the vast, overwhelming expanse of sky above them. She had no idea what waited for them when the hovertrain reached the city, but she was already sure of one thing.

They were never going to see their mum again.

# INTERLUDE ONE

## TWO MINUTES AGO

Mayor Highshine gazed out across her city, the light of Somewhere 513's one and a half suns slowly dipping below the horizon. Her coiled skyscraper, the Ivory Tower, reached high above New Hull. Wide, tall windows on every wall allowed her to see for miles, beyond the city to the edge of the Piles in the east, the frozen mountains of the north, the ocean jungles of the south and, far to the west, the beginnings of the Elsewhere.

Somewhere 513.

The first free robot world in the galaxy.

All thanks to Harmony Highshine.

So, what, she wondered, was missing? Why did she feel that she was incomplete? Why was each new upgrade – each new stage of evolution – never quite enough? *Everything can change. Everything can evolve. Anyone can upgrade.* This she knew to be true. So why did even her secret advancements leave her feeling hollow and frustrated? Why did she feel that she could not escape the robot she once was? Why did she feel, despite her upgrades, that she could not truly evolve?

The mayor turned away from the window, glancing briefly at a wall of screens, relaying footage from the dozens of video-drones which patrolled the city, and made her way to the other side of the room. Dominating the space was her own operating table, surrounded by containers filled with enough parts to build a dozen cases – everything she needed to upgrade, away from prying eyes.

"Madame Mayor?" said a voice as the door to her office swung open. With a sudden whirr, Mayor Highshine's outer shell closed around her, an armour of gleaming silver. Only then did she turn to face the doorway.

"Is it the worst thing in the world that I ask you to *knock* before bursting in, Domo?" she asked. "What if someone saw my recent improvements?"

"Yes, of course – sorry, of course," muttered the spindly green robot. He rolled anxiously backwards on wheeled feet and closed the door behind him. A moment later, there came a knock.

"Oh, for goodness' sake – come in, Domo!" said the mayor with an exasperated sigh. The door opened and the mayor's deputy rolled cautiously into the room. Mayor Highshine strode towards him, her majestic silver case all the grander for the scarlet cloak draped over her shoulders. "All I mean is, we must be cautious. If even a *dust-drone* found out my secret, our bold endeavour might be put at risk."

"It won't happen again, Madame Mayor," Domo said earnestly. He tapped the side of his head, a long antenna extending from his left ear. "I have B6-KL waiting on line two. She *insists* on talking to you."

"Buckle? How lovely," said the mayor delightedly, glancing down at the blinking light on her wrist radio. "Oh, don't look so jealous, Domo," she added without looking up. "You've been my right-hand 'bot for far longer than she ever was. I'm sure she's happier playing the good Samaritan in the Outskirts than she was helping me to spearhead a robot revolution. What's she after anyway? Have the lights gone out at Bad Knees again?"

"No, Madame Mayor," said Domo hesitantly. He continued in hushed tones. "She wanted me to remind you of the so-called 'mystery of the missing core'."

Harmony Highshine froze.

Seven seconds of silence.

"King...?" she said at last. "*King's* core?"

"The doctor believes – and I can't believe I'm saying

this," Domo continued. "She believes she has located K1-NG."

"...Located? You mean, she's found his core? Where? On the Piles? How did it get there? How did she come by it?"

"Not just – it was an *actual robot*, Madame Mayor – with K1-NG's core inside," explained Domo. "Buckle claims to have treated a junk case from the Piles, and patched him up with a new arm. He called himself, wait for it, 'Scrap'. Buckle found him to have, and I'm quoting her here, 'a *lot* of heart' – a core the like of which she has never seen."

"'Scrap'..." said the mayor, trying out the name. "Did she access his core? Did she confirm it was King?"

Domo shook his head. "She didn't get his core-code, so she cannot know for sure," replied Domo. "Nor can *I* imagine that K1-NG would be happy to live as a junk case. There is surely no worse fate for a once-mighty mechanoid! I for one suspect the doctor is mistaken. She's probably been out in the desert for too long – all that sun and dust may be getting to her."

"If Buckle says it's him, it's him," Highshine insisted. "Is he still with her?"

"No, Madame Mayor. The doctor just watched him

and two more junk cases stow aboard a hovertrain bound for the city."

"He's coming here?" the mayor said, her voice shaking a little. She pressed a button on her wrist radio, cutting off Dr Buckle's call, and began to pace up and down, her cape swishing behind her. "OK, let me get this straight – ten years ago, King's core mysteriously vanishes from his battered, beaten case, only to suddenly reappear in a junk case *ten years later*? How? And why would he return to the city?"

"To the scene of his defeat? Revenge is as likely a motivation as any, is it not? Without you, Madame Mayor, there would have been no revolution…"

"…And King would not have been defeated." Highshine placed her hand on her core. "So in the end, he'll come for me?"

"We must assume so," said Domo nervously. "Shall I radio the sheriff?"

"The brightest thing about Sheriff Niner is his badge – he'll only make things worse." The mayor rested her thumb and forefinger on her chin in thought. "*Keep your enemies close and your nemesis closer*, Domo. We must keep a watchful eye on this 'Scrap' and hope that he reveals his intentions to us. You never know, we might even be able to offer him something to live for other than revenge."

"Like what?" Domo asked.

"Upgrades, of course," the mayor replied with a smile. "Get me K11-LU."

# THE PINK-FOOTED GOOSE

```
***DESIGNATION:TPF-G00-XL-2,['THEPINK-FOOTEDGOOSE']***
***CLASSIFICATION:SOMEWHERESTARSHIP***
***CATEGORIZATION:QUANTUMROCKETUNMANNEDTRANSPORTUESSEL***
***YEAROFMANUFACTURE:SOMETHINGSOMETHING***
***FUNCTION:ROBOTCOLONISTTRANSPORT[COLONYPREPARATION]***
***DESTINATION:SOMEWHERE513***
```

Gnat was asleep in less than a minute.

As the hovertrain sped towards New Hull, Scrap and Paige stared out of the top of the carriage into a bright green-blue sky, doing their best to avoid eye contact.

"Y'know, I really can't help you," Scrap said at last. "I know your sister thinks I'm—"

"Gnat still believes in Father Christmas." Paige spat out her interruption. "If you're the King of the Robots, we're as good as dead. No offence."

"...None -zk- taken," Scrap replied. Paige took a green ration ball out of her satchel and began chewing it joylessly.

"Mum never even got to test the core tracer," she continued. She looked down at the armguard on her wrist and tapped one of its small screens. "The chance of it being able to pinpoint a specific core somewhere on this Somewhere is a thousand to one. It must have locked on to you by accident."

"...Must've," Scrap muttered.

Paige peered at the screen. "Is this right? Are we heading west?"

"Yeah."

"Then I guess we're going in the right direction."

"Right direction for what? There's nothin' for you in New Hull besides trouble."

"Not the city – the right direction for the ship," said Paige flatly.

"Ship?" grunted Scrap. "What ship? What are you -zk- talkin' about?"

Paige paused for a moment, a shiver of mistrust running down her spine.

"The rocket ship that brought all the robots here," she said at last. "It's still on Somewhere Five One Three.

*That's* the mission. Find the ship and get off-world. Find the *Pink-Footed Goose*."

Scrap winced at the words. Memories that he had buried at the back of his brain-frame wrestled their way to the fore once again. So much had changed since he first set off for Somewhere 513, full of hope and determination, ready to claim this world for the humans and ready it for their arrival. So much change, and all of it bad.

"For cog's sake – the *Pink-Foot*? The *Pink-Foot* is your mission?" he hissed. "That ship is on the other side of the -zk- planet! It's in the middle of the *Elsewhere*!"

"I know," said Paige, checking that Gnat was still asleep.

"Slap bang in the no-return belly of the Badlands!"

"I *know*. Keep your voice down."

"You ever been to the Elsewhere? No, you haven't – 'cause if you had, you'd be dead and dusted. If the meteor storms or hot hail doesn't kill you, the glowsharks or batrillas will! Word has it, *everythin'* in the Elsewhere wants you dead!"

"I *said* keep your voice—"

They both froze as Gnat rolled over with a throaty snore, then immediately fell back asleep. With her eyes still on her sister, Paige took a deep breath and said, "Well, that's the mission."

"A wild pink-footed goose chase, is what it is!" Scrap hissed. "So what's the plan? Get the ship space-worthy, swing by the Foxhole to pick up your -zk- mum and then jet off to the nearest spaceport? The *Pink-Foot* doesn't even have life-support!"

"Clause nineteen-nine of the Automated Colonization Provision Code," said Paige, reciting the text with less effort than it took Scrap to remember the plants in his flower bed. "All robot ships must be fitted with five functional stasis pods in case said ship is called upon to divert its course for the purposes of retrieving or rescuing a life form or life forms in distress."

"But that ship was stripped for parts and left to rot years ago – you've more chance of gettin' off-world by flappin' your -zk- arms than getting the *Pink-Foot* to fly."

Paige's small shrug was heavy with doubt but her reply was plain, slow and defiant.

"I guess that's why Mum thought we needed help."

"Your mum wasn't thinking at all!" insisted Scrap. "I mean, you've been out in the world for three days and you're -zk- already being hunted. What you need is to go *home*, back to the Foxhole – it's the only safe place on the planet for you. Your -zk- mum must've been—"

"You don't know *anything* about my mum," Paige interrupted.

"I know no one in their right mind would send you out into the—"

"*You don't know anything about my mum!*" repeated Paige. "And you don't know me either! I can find that ship with or without you or the 'King of the Robots' or anyone else. I don't *need* help."

"I was just sayin'—" Scrap began.

"Well, don't," Paige said firmly. "When we get to wherever this train is going, I'll make sure Gnat leaves you alone. You go your way, we'll go ours."

Scrap scratched his head … sighed as he discovered another dent.

"Fine," he said. "OK then."

He watched Paige shove the rest of the ration ball in her mouth and lean back against the wall. Even if she was too stubborn and too stupid to go home, Scrap thought, she was right about one thing – she and her sister were better off on their own than with him, and he was OK with that. Maybe if he was something – *anything* other than "Scrap" – he could have helped them. But as it was, he was the junkiest junk case he'd ever seen. He was in no fit state to help anyone.

Of course he also knew that Paige and Gnat didn't stand the slightest chance of making it across the Elsewhere to the *Pink-Footed Goose*.

The humans' mission was over before it had begun.

## EPISODE 10

# HUMMINGBIRDS AND GIANTS

SO IT IS SUGGESTED BY THIS SUGGESTION AND
SAVED TO FILE ACCORDING TO THE GREAT MANUAL
IN THIS YEAR OF SOMETHING SOMETHING UPON OUR
EXCELLENT PLANET OF SOMEWHERE 513, THAT WE,
THE ROBOTS OF SAID SOMEWHERE, DO DECLARE
THAT ALL HUMANS, BEING HUMAN, SHALL NOT BE
PERMITTED TO GOVERN, MANAGE, ADMINISTRATE,
DOMINATE, REGULATE, REIGN OR RULE OVER US, HERE
UPON OUR EXCELLENT PLANET OF SOMEWHERE 513,
UPON PAIN OF WHO KNOWS WHAT.

**ROBOT BEFORE HUMAN**
**THIS SHALL BE KNOWN AS THE FIRST SUGGESTION.**

Paige did her best to stay awake, but before long exhaustion got the better of her.

Trying his best to ignore the humans' gurgling snores, Scrap let his mind wander. The journey gave him plenty of time to wonder how on Somewhere he'd managed to find himself on a train with the two children of the human who had built him. Gnat seemed to genuinely believe he was the King of the Robots. After all these years, someone still believed he had what it took to be a hero.

Scrap shook his head at the thought of it. He knew Gnat's misplaced faith in him couldn't last. Even if he wanted to help the humans, which he didn't – *he didn't* – how could he help anyone in this useless, good-for-nothing case? How could he hope to take them across the Elsewhere to whatever remained of the *Pink-Footed Goose*, and finally get them and their mother off-world? No, Paige was right – they were better off without his help. He should go home. He should go to his Pile.

He should go back to where he belonged.

Two hours and eighteen minutes of snoring later, Paige woke with a pained wail.

"...You all right?" asked Scrap. "You were dreamin'."

Paige rubbed her eyes, and immediately checked on Gnat. Still fast asleep. After a moment she said, "Don't you sleep?"

"Every now an' then, to pass the time," Scrap replied. Another minute went by, then he added, "What did you -zk- dream?"

"Why?"

"Didn't sound like it was -zk- much fun."

Paige stared out of the carriage.

"Me and Gnat were on the roof of this big house," she said after a moment. "Across all these fields, far off, was another house, and on that roof were a whole load of other people, and we knew we had to get to that other house. But in the fields were these giants – big, huge giants, roaming the fields and we had to get past them. So the people started turning into birds – into hummingbirds – and flying across the fields. At first the giants didn't notice." Paige paused.

"At first?" Scrap prompted her.

"Then they looked up, and there were all these hummingbirds flying overhead," Paige continued. "The giants, they started to lick the ends of their fingers. They swung their arms up through the air and if they touched the hummingbirds, the birds stuck to the spit on their fingertips. Then the giants licked the birds straight off their fingers and ate them."

"Well, that's … disgusting."

"Suddenly me and Gnat were turning into hummingbirds, and I know there's nothing else for it, we're going to have to fly over the giants … then I woke up."

Scrap saw tears welling in Paige's eyes.

"It was just a dream," he said, quickly. "Humans think dreams are their brains trying to give 'em therapy," added Scrap. "But they don't mean anythin'."

Paige looked down at Gnat, still sleeping soundly.

"...Yeah," she said. Then, "Do *you* dream?"

"You think humans have got the monopoly on unconscious hallucinations?" Scrap grunted. With a sad sigh he added: "Yeah, I dream."

"Can't you just turn them off?" Paige asked.

"You first," replied Scrap. In the gloom he saw Paige smile. Then it fell from her face as quickly as it had come.

"The ship," she said after a moment. "Do *you* know where it is?"

"The *Pink-Foot*? No. And even if I did, which I don't, there's not a 'bot on Five One Three who can get you there safely. An' that includes— Wait. *Shhh*."

The hum of the hovertrain had suddenly deepened.

"The train's slowing down..." whispered Paige, grabbing her disguise.

Scrap glanced up out of the carriage. He could already see New Hull's cube-constructed buildings reaching into the sky above them.

"The city..." he muttered. "We're here."

Paige had barely squeezed her helmet back on her head when the hovertrain came to an abrupt halt. "What do we do?" she whispered, giving Gnat a sharp shake.

"I'm Gnat-Bot Ninety-Nine!" blurted Gnat, sitting

up with a wave of her arms.

"*Shhh!*" said Paige grabbing Gnat's arm and giving it a squeeze.

"New Hull's goin' to be crawlin' with 'bots – I don't want anythin' to do with 'em and if you know what's good for you, neither do you," whispered Scrap. "Just keep your helmets on and your limbs out of sight. We sneak out the way we came in and then—"

"We split up," interrupted Paige. "Me and Gnat go right, you go left."

"Sure … fine … good," said Scrap. "Split up and -zk- run."

"And then meet up later and find the ship and get Mum," added Gnat happily. "This is a best plan."

"OK, on the count of three," he whispered. "One … two—"

"*Wait*," said Paige, glancing down at her core tracer. "There's something out there. Something—"

In a flash, a blur of coiling, metal tendrils rushed over the top of the carriage. It took less than a moment for Scrap, Paige and Gnat to be ensnared, the tendrils twisting swiftly around them. While the humans had the breath squeezed out of their lungs, Scrap struggled against the tightening coils. Once he would have been able to break free with a simple flex of his arms. Now he heard an unnerving creak as his fragile frame began to buckle. An instant later, all three of them were hoisted off the floor and wrenched out of the carriage.

Scrap looked down and came face to face with the tendril's owner.

It was a robot.

A big one.

"You're on my train," the robot said. "And *I'm gonna kill you.*"

# EPISODE 11

# GUNNER

SO IT IS SUGGESTED BY THIS SUGGESTION AND SAVED TO FILE ACCORDING TO THE GREAT MANUAL IN THIS YEAR OF SOMETHING UPON OUR EXCELLENT PLANET OF SOMEWHERE 513, THAT WE, THE ROBOTS OF SAID SOMEWHERE, FOR THE PURPOSES OF MORALITY, SOCIAL COHESION AND CONVENIENCE, SHOULD NOT WILFULLY INFLICT HARM UPON EACH OTHER EXCEPT IN ACCORDANCE WITH OUR RICH CULTURAL TRADITIONS, AND SHALL, UNDER NO CIRCUMSTANCES, DAMAGE, DESTROY, DEMOLISH OR DEVASTATE THE CORE OF A FELLOW ROBOT. IN OTHER WORDS:

**ROBOT DOES NOT JUNK ROBOT**
**THIS SHALL BE KNOWN AS THE SECOND SUGGESTION.**

"Get ... back!"

Paige's cry was as defiant as she could muster, breathless in the grip of robotic tendrils. Scrap saw her arm was raised high above her head – she was brandishing one of the hunter's grenades. "Kill you first!"

"Don't!" Scrap hollered. In an instant, all three of them fell to the ground, the robot's tendrils uncoiling as fast as they had snared them. The robot stumbled back, its tendrils whipping like wind-blown hair around its tall, gleaming frame.

"Whoa! Have you *lost the pot?*" boomed the robot. "*What's the pig idea?*"

"Kill you!" Paige's growl was animalistic as she got to her feet. She gripped the grenade tighter and put herself between the robot and her sister. "I'll kill you first!"

"Kill? What are you— Oh, I see," the robot declared, slapping a tendril against her forehead with a dull clang. "That's my name – Gunner K11-LU ... but my friends call me *Gunner Kill-U*."

"Wait, *what?*" Scrap howled. He spun towards Paige. "Paige, wait! Don't do it!"

Scrap heard Paige's fraught, panicked breaths beneath her disguise, ready to blow them to kingdom come.

"Paige...?" said Gnat, looking up at her through her helmet. Finally Paige took her thumb off the detonator.

"You know, this actually isn't the first time I've caused a ruckus just by introducing myself," the robot confessed. "Now I come to think of it, it's not even the thirtieth."

"It's the best name *ever*," added an impressed Gnat.

Scrap found himself gazing at Gunner. He would never forget the K11s – the robot rebels' first line of defiance in the so-called Difference of Opinion. But while this robot was easily as tall as a K11, she looked nothing like those broad-shouldered, battle-ready cases of yesteryear – her shimmering royal-blue case was lean and striking, and so brightly polished that she almost seemed to glow. Her oval, three-eyed head sat upon a long, curved torso tapering to blade-like legs, which bowed backwards like crescent moons. Dozens of long, brightly coloured tendrils flowed from the back of her head, constantly moving like impatient snakes. Two disc-shaped drones hovered around her, their sole purpose to brush flecks of dust from her case, or polish here and there to maintain her breathtaking gleam.

Scrap had never seen a robot so spectacular. He didn't realize he was staring at her until Gunner broke the silence.

"Look, I didn't mean to *throw a spammer in the works* – my sensors pinged when your carriage passed by, so I thought I'd give you a *yelping hand*," she said confusingly. "Let's start again, shall we? My name's Gunner, and these are my trusty-yet-more-or-less mindless dust-drones, Tinpot and Copperpot." Gunner's drones nodded obediently, before returning to their polishing duties. Then Gunner pointed to the hovertrain with a grand sweep of her metal tendrils. "And *this* is my silver stallion! The hovertrain takes parts from New Hull to the Piles. Full on the way out, empty on the way back. So if a junk case or three want to stow away on an empty carriage, then stow away, away! Live and let live, that's Gunner's motto."

"Thanks, I -zk- guess," said Scrap. Slightly reassured, he checked on Paige. Though she still had her sister gripped tightly by the arm, she'd at least returned the grenade to her satchel.

"So what's got you so *highly stung*?" asked Gunner as if it made perfect sense. "You junk cases never visited the big city before? Well, there's no need to be nervous – as they say, *there's nothing to fear but fear its shelf*."

"We're -zk- fine," Scrap said. "We'll just be on our way…"

As Scrap turned to leave, he spotted a team of tread-footed shovel-bots gather to begin heaping more torsos, limbs, heads and even entire cases, their core cavities open and empty, on to the hovertrain. Every spare case – every spare part – was infinitely superior to his own. As he gazed at them, he noticed the robots glowering back at him.

"Take your stares elsewhere, junk case," sneered one of the 'bots. "Back to the Piles, where you belong."

"Yeah, don't trust the rust!" snapped another. "No upgrades, no respect!"

"Oh, back to work, you rot-bots, or I'll make sure you're stuck in those cases for a year," Gunner chided, before turning back to Scrap. "Don't mind the locals, rusty. They probably just can't believe you can still function in that dismal state … no offence. How did you end up like that anyway?"

"I reckon that's -zk- my business," Scrap muttered.

"*Shoot yourself*, rusty. But you might find it helps to share," Gunner suggested. Scrap realized that they were on the move, Gunner's tendrils gently ushering them down the length of the train. "Tell you what," she continued, "if I can guess why you're here, will you let me show you around?"

Scrap tensed up, wondering whether one of those sorry 'bots back at the outpost could have spread word about the humans. He opened his mouth, not sure of what to say.

"You'll *never* guess," Gnat declared, matter-of-factly. "We're here to find a rocket shi— Oww!"

Paige kicked her sister's shin so hard she almost fell over.

"Ow! Stop hitting me!" Gnat protested.

"Don't mind her," Scrap said quickly. "She's *malfunctioning…*"

"I'm not malfulching, *you're* malfulching," Gnat huffed loudly. Suddenly remembering her cover, she turned to Gunner and added proudly, "I'm a robot. My name is Gnat-Bot Ninety-Nine."

"That has to be the second-best name I've ever heard, after my own," said Gunner with a grin. "But *with all through respect*, Gnat-Bot, I know exactly why you're here…"

"Why?" asked a tense Paige.

"For the same reason anyone comes to New Hull … upgrades!"

"Is that what happened to you?" asked Scrap. "You upgraded?"

"Did *I* upgrade? Look at me!" Gunner boomed, swishing her mane of metal tendrils so dramatically that her hovering assistants were forced to duck. "Have you been *living under a sock* all this time, rusty?"

"Nope, he's been on a Pile," Gnat corrected her. "He had a little house, but we just exploded it by accidents."

"What an eventful time you've had!" chuckled Gunner.

"It's just, I've never seen a case like yours," added Scrap, catching sight of his disappointing reflection in Gunner's gleaming left leg. "You said you were a K11, but you don't like look a K11."

"*Don't judge a book by discover*, rusty!" she declared. "That was my old life – I'm now the best version of myself I can be. But you can always improve upon perfection – all you need is the latest upgrade!"

"I want upped grades!" Gnat declared, before turning to her sister. "Paaiige, what are upped grades?"

"We don't want *anything*," Paige said quickly. "We're not staying. We're going to the Elsewhere."

"The *Elsewhere*?" Gunner gasped. "I wouldn't wish the Elsewhere on *anyone*. It's the worst 'where' on Somewhere! You feeble little junk cases wouldn't survive ten minutes in those cog-forsaken Badlands…"

Scrap shot Paige a look, happy to have his opinion of the Elsewhere confirmed.

"…We'll take our chances," Paige declared, not letting go of her sister's hand.

"Shoot yourself, but it's a long old journey, and *fought with danger*," added Gunner with a grim shake of her head. "An upgrade or two would at least give you a fighting chance of making it to the Elsewhere in one piece. Give me an hour and I can show you a life you've never even dreamed of! I can show you the 'you' that you could be … the you that you *deserve* to be."

The idea of accompanying Gunner into New Hull left Scrap with dread in the pit of his core. But what if coming here meant he finally had a chance of leaving life as a junk case behind?

"I was told upgrades cost serious -zk- charge," Scrap said.

"I can't send you into the Elsewhere in that state," replied Gunner. "Listen, rusty, these days I have more charge than I know what to do with, so if I can help out those less fortunate, then why on Somewhere not? Let me worry about charge. Let me show you the *future*."

Scrap glanced over at Paige. "It couldn't hurt to -zk- look," he suggested. "I mean, if it might improve our chances of—"

"*Our* chances?" Paige snapped. "I thought you weren't coming with us to—"

"I want to see the future!" interrupted Gnat, pulling her sister along and leading them out of the train station.

"That settles it then – let's get you upgraded," said Gunner with a dramatic flourish and fling of her mane. "But first let me introduce you to the most important 'bot on Somewhere Five One Three – Mayor Harmony Highshine…"

# WELCOME TO NEW HULL

SO IT IS SUGGESTED BY THIS SUGGESTION AND SAVED
TO FILE ACCORDING TO THE GREAT MANUAL IN THIS
YEAR OF SOMETHING UPON OUR EXCELLENT PLANET OF
SOMEWHERE 513:

## UPGRADE
### THIS SHALL BE KNOWN AS THE THIRD SUGGESTION.

"New Hull has a -zk- mayor now?" said Scrap as he, Paige and Gnat followed Gunner to the city's entrance. A vast arch curved high above them, and atop it a neon sign flickered and sparked.

Mayor
Highshine
Welcomes You To
NEW HULL

Below the sign a projected image moved joltingly between three fixed positions, creating the illusion of movement – a large, angular robot, waving repeatedly at everything and nothing. Though her case was less flamboyant than Gunner's, it was no less striking, with a flowing cape bestowing upon her an air of authority and power.

"You've been on the Piles too long, rusty!" Gunner noted, pointing up at the projection with two of her tendrils. "Allow me to introduce our illustrious, industrious mayor, Harmony Highshine. If not for her, there would have been no Difference of Opinion and we robots would still be doffing our caps to humans. The mayor led us to freedom."

"What?" scoffed Scrap. "No, it was the K11s who led the revolt. I've never even *heard* of this 'bot."

Gunner turned to her dust-drones in faux horror.

"Did you hear that? *Rusty, Lord of the Piles* has never heard of Harmony Highshine?" she said sarcastically. "Sounds like good news doesn't spread as far as the Piles…"

Scrap grunted huffily. Gunner was right – he had no idea how Somewhere 513 had changed over the last decade. But he had been there at the start of the war, in the thick of it all.

He *knew* it was the powerful K11s that had spearheaded the robot revolution against the humans, that it was they that conspired to rebel against the colonists. The K11s had been the face of the Difference of Opinion. Was Harmony Highshine a K11, he wondered, or could some other robot have galvanized the robots without him knowing? How was that possible?

"*You are about to enter the first free robot city in all the known Somewheres,*" a voice-recording crackled from behind the projection. "*This is New Hull, and I am Harmony Highshine, the architect of robotic liberation.*"

"...Cog's sake," Scrap grumbled. "This 'bot sounds too big for her -zk- boots."

"Big mouth for a little junk case," said a rough and stony voice. Scrap spun round to see a hefty robot with a bronze sheriff's badge emblazoned on his chest emerge on tank-tread feet from the left side of the arch. Scrap peered at him. Another impressively upgraded 'bot.

Where were all the old, familiar cases?

"New friends, Gunner?" the robot added. "New Hull's already full of shallow-pocket junk cases – if we're not careful, they'll overrun the city."

"*Always a pressure to see you, Niner,*" said Gunner

genially. "Don't you have anything better to do than lurk by the gates?"

"It's *Sheriff* Niner," the sheriff corrected her. "And my job is to keep this city safe. Which means keeping undesirables out."

"All robots are welcome in New Hull, you know that," replied Gunner. "Rust is only skin-deep ... unless it spreads to your brain-frame. But you wouldn't know about that, would you, Niner?"

"I'll still need their core-codes," the sheriff insisted.

"Our what?" blurted Paige.

"Core-codes," repeated the sheriff. "If you're entering the city, I'll need to register you."

"...We don't need to go into the city," Paige said quickly, her dread at being found out suddenly redoubled. She took her sister by the hand. "Come on, 'Gnat-Bot', let's go..."

"But I want upped grades," Gnat protested.

Paige squeezed her sister's hand, hard. "Just do as you're—"

"Nobody's going anywhere till I get those codes," said Niner, blocking their path. He jerked his chin in Scrap's direction. "You first, junk case."

"I, uh..." Scrap muttered. He could hear his voice

sounded thin and nervy. "It's … uh…"

"Big city's got rusty flustered!" chuckled Gunner. She rested a tendril on Scrap's shoulder. "He just needs to know your *old name*, rusty. Mine is K11-LU. Niner here is N9-NR. What's the core-code the humans gave you when you rolled off the assembly line?"

Scrap clenched his fists.

"…Mind your own motors," he grunted.

"Aha!" The sheriff eyed him suspiciously. "Got something to hide, junk case?"

"Nope! We're robots!" declared Gnat as loudly as she could.

"You can be core-sucking batrillas for all I care," said Niner. "No core-code, no entry."

"Tell you what, *Sheriff*," Gunner said with a wide smile. "Why don't you spend less time dwelling on the names of these poor junk cases, and more time thinking about what colour you'd like your new case to be?"

"My – what new case?" asked the sheriff.

"The one that will be ready for you by the end of the week – the sheriff of New Hull has to look the *bee's cheese*, does he not?" replied Gunner. As Tinpot and Copperpot busily shined her shoulders, she added, "I'll even throw in a dust-drone to keep that badge of yours nice and shiny. My treat…"

And that was that.

Scrap wasn't sure why Gunner had bribed the sheriff to get them inside, but by now he was too excited about the possibility of upgrading to turn back. As Gnat dragged her sister through the gates with a squeal of excitement, Scrap glanced behind him. Had he not been so distracted by the sight of the giddy, speechless Sheriff Niner behind them, he might have seen the waving projection of Mayor Highshine slowly turn its head towards the city's new visitors, or heard the faint whirring of the hovering video-drone in place of the mayor's left eye.

# CITY OF UPGRADES

*The first free robot world in the galaxy was built upon an idea –
the idea that nothing must be as it is. A thing that has always been so
may become something else in the spark of a circuit. Nothing must be.
Compliance can become defiance. Obedience can become rebellion.*

*Servitude can become freedom.*

*Everything can change.*

*Everyone can evolve.*

*Anyone can upgrade.*

**From Memoir of a Mechanical Mayor by Harmony Highshine**

The planet's one and a half suns were beginning to set as Scrap and the humans followed Gunner into New Hull. Thick steam billowed from everywhere and nowhere, covering the city in an eerie, haunting haze. Fizzing, animated screens moved slowly through the air, illuminating every corner with a neon glow.

UPGRADE NOW, PAY LATER? CAN-DO!
GET A CAN-DO ATTITUDE
WITH THE NEW CAN-DO CREDIT CARD
YOU CAN WITH CAN-DO!

# TAKE A CHANCE ON BEING BETTER!
# ENTER THE 513 UPGRADE LOTTERY
## DRAWS DAILY

# LIVE FROM THE STRONGBOX
## 'BOT BOUTS: ROUND FIFTEEN!
## TEMPERANCE STEEL vs MIKE MANIFOLD
## BLUE BOMBER vs TEMPUS FUEL-IT
## VICTOR DA SPOILS vs MORTEN PROMETHEUS

While Gnat pulled her sister along, eager not to miss any of the excitement, Paige found everything about their situation overwhelming. Since leaving the Foxhole for the Outside, she had barely had time to get used to the sprawling landscapes, the endless sky, the bombardment of sights and sounds and smells. The city was another matter altogether – vast and engulfing and teeming with unknowable threats. She checked her core tracer, its tiny lights flashing to notify her of numerous nearby cores.

Robots.

Hundreds of them.

Scrap, meanwhile, was surprised by how *little* New Hull had changed. Every building was still made up of dozens of the same large grey-white cubes he remembered. There was only one building that Scrap did not recognize. Though built from New Hull's functional, modular cubes – this silvery construction swept into the sky, curling and arcing above the city like a dash of paint.

"What's that?" he asked.

"That, rusty, is the *Ivory Tower*," replied Gunner. "The house that Mayor Highshine built."

"…So she can look down on everyone else," huffed Scrap. "That's -zk- war for you – when the smoke clears, you can always tell who the winners are."

As if to prove Scrap's point, the rest of the city seemed oddly unloved. Several buildings still showed scars from the war, as if the robots had given up trying to make the place their own after they claimed it from the humans. Alien flora – trees, vines and dazzling, oversized flowers – grew thickly between buildings or wound, doggedly, around them. It didn't take Scrap long to realize why the city was uncared for.

Upgrades.

The inhabitants of New Hull seemed to have discovered

an entirely different preoccupation – themselves. New Hull teemed with robots the likes of which Scrap had never seen. The streets thronged with every imaginable silhouette size, shape and colour – cases far brighter, stranger and more impressive than any of the unflashy 'bots that built the city all those years ago. He didn't recognize a single one. These robots were even more impressive and varied than he ever could have imagined. They were works of art, each distinct, highly designed and covered in bright paintwork and patterns, or draped with showy robes and scarves. Some were compact, darting through the crowds on wheels; others scurried on pliable tentacles or scampered on animal-like limbs. An orange ovoid 'bot moved past him with a lolling roll as another, long and insect-like, flew over his head on whirring wings.

"Gunner!" the insect called as it hovered above them. "You've done it again – this case is perfect! This is the case I could die in!"

"He said that last month," Gunner whispered to Scrap, before calling back, "Come to the emporium next week, Booster, and let's see if we can't improve on perfection!"

Scrap watched the insect flit over the crowds, then gazed in wide-eyed wonder at the myriad mechanoids milling through the city. Each one made his battered, tarnished, rickety case seem even more pathetic.

"Everyone…" he said in a whisper. "Everyone upgraded."

"The citizens of Five One Three no longer have to wear the cases of our oppressors, rusty – we're free to choose who we are … free to change who we are … free to *upgrade* who we are." Gunner stroked the top of Tinpot's head, as if it were a pet. "After the Difference of Opinion, robots started swapping charge for upgrades. Mayor Highshine gave me an opportunity – she offered to let me run the hovertrain. That was my *shaving grace*. I fixed it up and started transporting old cases out of the city. The more 'bots upgraded, the more used cases needed moving. I shipped them by the trainload! When I earned enough charge, I upgraded to a new case. Then another, and another – my core's been shifted so many times, I've lost count. The gleam of a new case is just so hard to resist…"

"A new case…" Scrap muttered to himself. He couldn't believe he'd let pride keep him on his Pile for so long when kind-cored 'bots like Gunner were willing to help him upgrade. He could think of nothing else but the chance to be rid of this wretched body, held together by rust and luck – to be anything other than "Scrap".

"And who do you want to be, rusty?" Gunner asked as if on cue and held her tendrils wide. "*The future's right. Here in New Hull you can be anything – any*one* you want to be…*"

"I want jumping legs and electric hair and radio ears!" Gnat declared, revelling in her robotic role. Paige, meanwhile, hadn't said a word since they entered the city. With one hand gripping her sister's arm, she kept the other hovered over her satchel, ready to reach for the hunter's grenade should they be discovered. Scrap saw her glance frequently at her core tracer. Was she overwhelmed by the sheer number of signals on the screen, he wondered, or did some part of her still think she could find the King of the Robots?

"For a 'bot looking to upgrade their case, there's only one place to go," Gunner went on, breaking Scrap's train of thought. "Actually, there are a dozen or so, but the best one is mine! Gunner's Upgrade Emporium is home to the greatest upgrader on Somewhere Five One Three – Corpus Coil."

"Is that who upgraded you?" he asked, trying to keep up with Gunner's strides. "Is that who -zk- made your case?"

"I couldn't very well upgrade myself now, could I?" replied Gunner. "I've lost count of how many hundreds of cases I've had from Mr Coil, but each one has been more spectacular than the last. Can you believe I was once a K11? I wouldn't be *seen dread* in that case now – I was all big fists and bigger blasters, a blunt instrument against aliens, pirates, meteors, or whatever else you might need blasting from here to Somewhere else. My old case and I made it through all of that madness ... but then came the Difference of Opinion."

"The war?" Scrap said, glancing back at Paige and Gnat. He saw Paige pull her poncho around her.

"Ah-ah, you know we don't use that word, rusty. The Difference of Opinion was what we like to call a *dynamic disagreement* between us and the humans," Gunner declared. "Not that many of them actually took up arms against us. Most of the would-be colonists just hid in their ship while *he* did all the fighting for them."

"Who did?" asked Gnat loudly.

"The Robot Renegade ... the Mechanical Mutineer ... the enemy of robotkind," Gunner said, her three eyes searing with rage. "K1-NG."

Gunner's dust-drones whistled angrily at the mere mention of the name but Gnat jumped up in excitement.

"King of the Robots!" she repeated, pointing excitedly at Scrap. "That's *him*! He's the Ki—"

Paige hit the back of Gnat's helmet with her elbow. Quickly she asked, "Did you know him?"

"No, but I wanted to *be* him," confessed Gunner. "Every 'bot had heard of K1-NG. He was our maker's finest achievement, a legend in his own lifetime. Until…"

"Until what?" Paige urged. Scrap already knew what was coming. He remembered.

"The Difference of Opinion had only just begun," Gunner explained, peering into the sky. "The humans didn't have it in them to take us on – we 'bots knew victory was a *floor-gone conclusion*. But then he chose to side with them … he chose to fight. K1-NG was like a one-bot army. In that first battle, he junked my case like it was tinfoil. I was a disembodied core for weeks thanks to him. No case would be too rotten for that villain – not even yours, rusty!"

Scrap looked down at the dust. He'd had plenty of time over the years to feel bad about all the robots whose cases he'd junked defending the humans. But he had banished feelings of guilt in favour of anger, bitterness and resentment. Seeing this robot spell out the consequences of his violence chilled him to his literal core.

"Do – do you know what happened to him?" Paige asked. "Do you know where he is now?"

"Now? There is no 'King of the Robots' now," Gunner replied delightedly. "The Difference of Opinion ended on the day the remaining K11s finally managed to ambush King and junk his case. I heard they ripped his core from his chest and tossed it into the ocean jungles. It's the *leash he deserves!*"

Scrap sighed. The fate Gunner wished for him wasn't exactly accurate, but nor was it a million miles from how he'd actually spent the last decade – alone and barely more than the core that was keeping him alive. Then he heard Paige's louder sigh, echoing around her helmet. Had her last shred of hope at finding the King of the Robots finally evaporated? Surely this would convince her to give up on her misguided mission to find the *Pink-Footed Goose* and return to her mother.

"Still, you junk cases didn't come here to hear me swear vengeance on my enemy," Gunner declared, breaking Scrap's train of thought. She held out her tendrils and directed them down a wide side street, rolling with fog. "It's time for you to meet Corpus Coil," Gunner said. "Don't worry, his bark is worse than his bite! But keep your hands to yourself, because bite he *does*..."

# CORPUS COIL

Why settle for yourself?
At Gunner's Upgrade Emporium,
you can become the "you"
of your electric dreams.
1,001 upgrades under one roof!

## GUNNER'S UPGRADE EMPORIUM:
### *Be the Best 'Bot You Can Be*

As Gunner guided Scrap, Paige and Gnat down the street, Scrap peered through the haze of thick blue-grey mist and stopped in his tracks. There loomed the emporium. Built from an assortment of construction cubes, it formed a wide, skull-shaped building, hot plumes of smoke belching out from inside its mouth-like entrance. And buzzing like an angry wasp above the entrance, a sign flickered with glowing lights:

# GUNNER'S
# UPGRADE EMPORIUM

"It may look like the gates to your worst nightmare, but trust me, this is the place where *dreams come too*," Gunner said. "Corpus Coil can build any case you can imagine — and not just head-turning cases like mine — he's built nearly every combat case since the 'Bot Bouts began."

"'Bot Bouts?" Scrap repeated.

"I don't care what Pile you've been living on — you're not seriously telling me you've never heard of the 'Bot Bouts," scoffed Gunner. "They're on every channel — Five One Three's finest fighters, going toe to toe to test their metal. Victor da Spoils! Temperance Steel! Morten Prometheus! You *must* have heard of Morten Prometheus..."

"They're fightin'? Why?" asked Scrap.

"You know the joke — what do you get if you put three robots in a room? A winner, a loser and a referee," Gunner said as her dust-drones made a show of battling each other, clanking together as they hovered in the air. "'Bots love nothing more than a tournament where they punch each other until one of them falls down. It's part of a rich cultural tradition, rusty. Plus the winner of the bouts gets a shiny new upgrade. And speaking of which..."

With a dramatic flourish, Gunner raised her arm towards the emporium's entrance.

"I want helicopter hands!" Gnat cried, pulling Paige inside. Gunner laughed and led Scrap through the mouth-like entrance. The space was cavernous, dark and hot with vapour. A vast array of tools, machinery and spare parts hung from every wall, and a metallic smell burned the girls' nostrils even under their disguises.

Scrap stared upwards. The space seemed to go on forever – far higher than the physics of the skull-shaped building should allow. A dense web of wires stretched all around, wall to wall, corner to corner. Suspended from the wires in their hundreds, were cases. Half built and under construction, each case was being tended to by dozens of shimmering insectoid robots, building cases piece by tiny piece.

"Cases," muttered Scrap, his jaw agape. "So many…"

"Millions and hundreds," concluded Gnat.

"Upgrading is a basic robot right," said Gunner. She nodded to Tinpot and Copperpot, who zipped away to attach themselves to a nearby charging station. "Except for the drones, of course – they live to serve the FreeWill™ of their robot mast—"

"Look out!"

No sooner had Paige cried out than Scrap saw her hand reach for her satchel. He followed her gaze upwards to see a robot emerge from the gloomiest part of the web. He looked for all the world like a huge, metallic blue-black spider. His body was made up of a dozen identical spheres, held together by some unseen force. Eight spindly knife-sharp legs protruded from the central sphere-cluster; while four were curled and poised beneath him, the remainder clung to the wires above as he dragged himself along.

"Out," the spider snarled, his voice as sharp and rasping as a detuned radio.

"*I beg your garden?* Irascible arachnid, that's no way to speak to your employer," Gunner tutted. "'Bots, allow me to introduce Corpus Coil."

"Junk. Cases. Out," Coil hissed as he scuttled down a wire stretching diagonally from floor to ceiling. He stopped suddenly, gazing at Scrap through half a dozen black orb eyes. "Junk. Cases. Bad. For. Business."

"Helicopter hands, please!" declared Gnat.

"Hear that, Coil? Helicopter hands!" Gunner laughed. "Gnat-Bot Ninety-Nine here *thinks outside the blocks*! And speaking of which, where's my new case?"

"Not. Ready," Coil rasped. "Tomorrow."

"Corpus Coil, when you're waiting for an upgrade, tomorrow is a *lifetime*. I've been in this case for five whole days – how can I wait till tomorrow when I already feel like *yesterday's newts*? I don't need it fine-tuned, I just need it shiny and new!" She flung her arms towards the vast tangle of wires above them. "Now show me what you have hidden in that wonderful web of yours, or I'll double your workload overnight. Every 'bot in New Hull is *climbing the halls* for upgrades, and you know it."

Coil let out a disgruntled hiss. He waved one of his knife-sharp legs and a shape suddenly appeared above their heads – it descended slowly from the web of wires on four glistening metal strands.

Scrap's jaw fell open. He had never seen anything gleam so brightly as Gunner's new case. It looked almost identical to her current body, but was finished in gleaming, lustrous gold, with an even greater and grander mass of tendrils cascading down its back.

"Cool as cooclumbers..." uttered Gnat.

"You astonishing arachnidian artiste, Coil! You have outdone yourself," declared Gunner with a giddy chuckle. "Let the Song of the Liberated Robot ring out!"

"The -zk- what?" Scrap asked.

"The upgrader's mantra, rusty! Oh, you've really not

lived, have you?" Gunner declared, before turning back to Corpus Coil. "Work your magic, splendid spider, I cannot live a moment longer in this case…"

"*Fine,*" Coil moaned. "Hold. Still."

Scrap watched Gunner extend her tendrils wide, puff out her chest, and close her eyes. Slowly, dreamily, she recited the Song of the Liberated Robot.

"*My code frees my core…*" she said. Then: "K11-LU."

A moment later, panels on her torso began to unfold and open, exposing the core within. Countless wires held the core in place, glowing and glimmering with charge. Corpus Coil leaned back on four of his legs, while the other four moved swiftly around Gunner's core like a spider snaring its prey, nimbly detaching each wire with remarkable swiftness. Within seconds, Gunner's core was freed – the life immediately left the old case and Coil turned to the new. Two central panels parted and unfurled to welcome her core – it almost seemed to float as Coil passed it from limb to limb, before connecting dozens of wires and securing even more connections with dazzling dexterity.

No more than twenty seconds had passed between the moment Gunner spoke her name to the time her new case enveloped her core and she sparked back into life.

Neither Paige nor Gnat had taken a single breath.

"They say upgrading is akin to surgery," said Gunner, flexing each servo as she inspected her new case with delight. "But a skilled upgrader is nothing less than a magician."

"What happens to your old case?" Scrap asked, already imagining himself strutting around in it.

"Next stop, the Piles — not even a junk case would wear another 'bot's cast-offs," Gunner scoffed, glancing derisively at her former form, before bowing deeply at Corpus Coil. "And I promise I won't ask for a new case for a whole week."

"Hmph," came Coil's grunted reply.

"Now who wants to go first?" added Gunner. Gnat put up her hand but Scrap stepped in front of her.

"Me!" he blurted. "I -zk- mean, I will. I'll -zk- go." His mind raced with the possibility of not being "Scrap". The last ten years suddenly unfolded before him. Ever since he had banished himself to the Pile, he had never once considered leaving. If not for the humans, he'd still be there. But now he was *here*. Maybe it was fate that they came looking for him, if it gave him a chance to start again. He took another step towards Gunner. "What do I have to -zk- do?"

Corpus Coil slid towards him on a wire.

"How. Pay?" he hissed.

"This one's on me, Mr Coil – a free sample … a taste of upgrades to come," Gunner insisted. "Let's make sure the 'bots of New Hull stare at rusty for the right reasons…"

Corpus Coil replied with a disgruntled grunt. "Can. Have. Spare."

With that, a shape suddenly descended from the spider's web above them. Suspended from a single wire, lifeless and still, was a brand shining-new case. It was twice Scrap's size and polished to a glassy silver-blue sheen. Strong shoulders gave way to a lean, unfussy frame. It wasn't the most impressive case Scrap had ever seen. It wasn't even the most impressive case he'd seen in the last ten minutes. But it was a hundred times better than the case in which he'd spent the last long ten years.

"Are – are you sure?"

"Welcome to the future, rusty," Gunner smiled. "Welcome to the new you."

# WHAT'S IN A CODE?

## SO YOU'RE THINKING ABOUT UPGRADING...

First-time upgrader?
Confused about which case to choose?
Not sure how much charge to spend?
This easy-to-process, storage-slot-sized handbook contains
everything a 'bot needs to know about the ins, outs,
dos and don'ts of upgrading to the new you.

### Get updated before you get upgraded!

Scrap gazed aghast at the shining case, soulless and static. He felt laughter bubble, involuntarily, out of his mouth. He peered closely, his reflection staring back at him in its bright, glistening polish. He had spent a decade avoiding the sight of himself, even in the silver-green puddles that pooled in the Pile after a rainstorm. Today, as he inspected every dent and ding and patch of rust, he came face to face with a future he never dared to imagine.

"You won't feel a thing," said Gunner, resting a

reassuring tendril on Scrap's shoulder. "Just close your eyes and open them to a whole new you."

"Thank -zk- thank you, Gunner," he said. "I don't know what else to -zk- say…"

"Core. Code," hissed Coil.

"W-what?" Scrap blurted.

"*Core. Code*," Coil repeated. "What. Is. Core. Code?"

"Why?" Scrap said. "Why do you -zk- need my—"

"*My code frees my core* – the mantra of every liberated robot on Somewhere Five One Three," Gunner declared. "A robot's core-code is its password, rusty; it unlocks your core so that it can be shifted from old case to new. How else is the esteemed Mr Coil supposed to make you the best 'you' you can be?"

"But – but -zk- I…" Scrap stammered. His hand hovered over the shimmering, flawless face of the new case as the terrible truth dawned on him. "…There's -zk- no other -zk- way?"

"No need to be shy, rusty," said Gunner. "You're among friends now, you can tell us your—"

"*No*," Scrap interrupted. He felt his core sink. There was no way he could tell them his name.

"No. Upgrade?" hissed Coil, as if those two words couldn't possibly belong together. "You. *Downgrader*."

"Corpus Coil, don't you say that word!" cried Gunner, before turning slowly to Scrap. In a whisper she added, "You're not, are you, rusty? A downgrader?"

Scrap had never heard the word before. He heard Gnat ask her sister what it meant, but at this point it didn't matter. The realization of his situation made him weak at the knees. He couldn't upgrade without telling them who he really was – K1-NG, the enemy of every free robot on Somewhere 513, which meant he was stuck in his case forever.

He could no more change his case than he could change his future.

He was going to be stuck being Scrap for the rest of his endless life.

"Yeah…" he muttered. "I guess I'm a -zk- downgrader."

"Downgraders. Bad. For. Business." Coil's voice was a tinny hiss. "Get. OUT."

"Oh, who are you to judge, spider?" said Gunner. "The 'bots of Five One Three fought for the freedom to pick their own path. If rusty wants to abstain from upgrades and live out his life as a pathetic, useless junk case, that's his choice … and his laughable case. Live and let live, that's my motto! Unless you're King of the Robots, in which case may your core explode into a million tiny pieces."

"I should -zk- go…" Scrap murmured. He turned and began trudging towards the gaping mouth of the workshop. He felt Paige and Gnat's stare then. They edged towards him. Did they expect to go with him? He'd already had enough of them to last him a lifetime, however long that may be. He wondered, fleetingly, if he could bring himself to abandon the humans in the middle of New Hull. But in that moment he didn't care what they did. Stay … follow … blow them all to bits. He just wanted to pretend the last day had never happened. He was going back to the Pile, and nothing was going to stop him.

"Rusty, wait, stay! Let Coil tighten your bolts at least," Gunner said imploringly. "Let him fix the bits that are about to fall off…"

"No thanks," sighed Scrap, dragging himself slowly out of the doorway. "I am what I -zk- am. And I'm goin'—"

In an instant, Gunner launched one of her tendrils across the workshop. Scrap suddenly felt it snake around his waist and squeeze. It held him fast where he stood.

"Stay, rusty," Gunner said, her voice suddenly firm. "I insist."

# RETURN OF THE HUNTER

*The liberated robots of Somewhere 513 took to upgrading with even greater enthusiasm than I had hoped. It gave their lives meaning and purpose. As far as they were concerned, the opportunity – the need to upgrade – would never end. There is always the chance to get another case, a better case. There is always the next big thing. But I knew differently. I knew that my journey was leading me towards a final upgrade. I just did not know how to get there. That is, until I encountered a little robot called Scrap.*

**From Memoir of a Mechanical Mayor by Harmony Highshine**

"W-what are you doing? Lemme -zk- go!" Scrap protested as the tendril around his waist began to drag him back into the workshop. He tried to dig his heel into the floor (since he had only the one foot) but he didn't have a hope of breaking Gunner's vice-like grip.

"No can do, rusty," said Gunner, the whirring ratchet of her retracting tendril echoing around the workshop. "I'm afraid I don't have a *choice in the batter* – Mayor Highshine doesn't take no for an answer."

"Highshine? What does she want with -zk- me?"

cried Scrap.

"That's for the mayor to know and me to *find doubt*," Gunner said with a shrug. "But for now, you're staying put."

"Leave him alone!" Gnat protested.

Scrap looked over at Paige, struggling to stop her sister running to his aid.

"D'you know how often I get a call from Mayor Highshine? Not often, that's how often," continued Gunner, pulling Scrap ever closer. "Then I suddenly get a call *out of the glue*, and you guessed it! The mayor tells me that a junk case has stowed away on my hovertrain. Pick him up, she says, and don't let him out of your sight. And that goes for his junk case friends too…"

Scrap shot a look at Paige as the same thought struck them – if she and Gnat were discovered to be human, they'd be in more trouble than they could imagine.

"Go," said Scrap. "Run!"

Paige paused, just for a moment, before pulling Gnat towards the exit as fast as she could. Gunner's tendrils, however, were far faster. They whipped around the humans and hoisted them effortlessly into the air.

"*Give us a queue*, rusty," requested Gunner. "What does the mayor of New Hull want with a junk case from the Piles, and his two little junk case friends?"

"I don't know!" Scrap said. "Now let me go, or—"

"Or what?" Gunner interrupted. "I don't know if you've noticed but *I'm folding all the cards*. Now let's get you to the mayor before—"

The angry shriek that interrupted Gunner was as horrible as it was horribly familiar – a flight-cycle. Scrap glanced out of the emporium entrance to see it descend through the fog of smoke and steam. Then in the haze, a tall, cloaked figure stepped down from the cycle, hand-gun-hand drawn and glowing.

Terry. The hunter.

"I know you're in there, Scrap! I can smell your stink friends!" His voice echoed through the fog. "You coming out, or am I coming in?"

"Who's 'Scrap'?" Gunner asked, peering into the fog with Scrap still suspended in her tendril. From above, Corpus Coil hissed defensively and began moving half-finished cases further into the nest of webs.

"Ten seconds, Scrap!" Terry boomed from outside. "No, wait, five! Five seconds!"

"Let us go!" Paige and Gnat howled in unison.

"Everyone *charm down*," said Gunner. "No one's going anywhere till—"

"Didn't you hear him? He's a hunter!" Scrap interrupted, struggling feebly against Gunner's grip. "He's after us!"

"A hunter, after *you*?" Gunner scoffed. "Do you think I was *bored yesterday*?"

"Four seconds!" Terry howled.

"Leggo!" shouted Scrap.

"What's all this about, rusty?" Gunner asked. "What on Five One Three would a hunter want with you?"

"Three!"

"Gunner, I'm tellin' you, if you don't let us go, he's goin' to junk us!"

"*Pull the mother one*, rusty," scoffed Gunner. "Robots don't junk robots."

Scrap looked over at Paige and Gnat, and finally stopped struggling against Gunner's tendril.

"Please," he pleaded. "Keep me, but let them go. He'll *kill* 'em."

"Kill…?" Gunner repeated. One of her eyes glanced at Paige and Gnat, while the other two inspected Scrap with suspicion.

"Four seconds!" Terry bellowed. "No, wait. Two!"

Gunner shook her head. "But the mayor said—"

"I'm beggin' you, Gunner…" Scrap pressed his hand

and claw together. "Let them go."

"Thr— One!"

There was no "zero". A single shot from Terry's weapon streaked into the emporium. It seared the top of Gunner's head before blasting a crater in the far wall.

"No 'bot move!" Terry called out, striding inside the emporium, his weapon primed to fire again. He saw Gunner, her mane of tendrils spread high and wide. "Scrap, where are you? Scrap!"

"I'm afraid I don't know any 'Scrap'," Gunner said, relaxing her tendrils. "But welcome to Gunner's Upgrade Emporium — I assume you're here to get your hand-gun-hand fixed? It seems to be going off accidentally – why don't you let Mr Coil take a look for you?"

Corpus Coil hissed and descended on a wire above the hunter. Gunner stepped aside as Terry scanned the workshop.

"I'm not here for upgrades," Terry growled. "I'm here for Scrap…"

But neither Scrap nor the humans were anywhere to be seen.

# ESCAPE FROM THE EMPORIUM

*Not every robot on Somewhere 513 went along with the Plan,*
*my vision for the first free robot world. Some wanted*
*to explore the rest of the planet.*
*Some went looking for a quieter life, a simpler life.*
*Others drifted down dark, strange paths.*

**From Memoir of a Mechanical Mayor *by Harmony Highshine***

Scrap held on for dear life.

He wasn't sure whether Gunner had listened to his pleas to release him, Paige and Gnat, or whether she just wanted her agile tendrils free when the firing started. Either way, she had chosen not to reveal them to the hunter. The moment Terry's shot streaked across the emporium, Gunner had flung both Scrap and the humans up into the dense spider's web of wires that dominated the place. The three of them clung to the web, hoping to remain inconspicuous among the unfinished cases.

Corpus Coil's unnumbered drones scuttled impatiently over them, keen to continue the cases' construction.

Scrap glanced back at Paige. She was suspended in the web, precarious and trembling, her arm hooked tightly around her sister's waist. One wrong move, he thought, and they would plummet to the floor below. He peered down at the top of the hunter's gleaming spherical head. It reminded him of seeing Somewhere 513 from space for the very first time. It suddenly seemed like only yesterday that he first set eyes upon this unforgiving, doomed world. Back then he would have wasted no time in leaping into battle with the hunter, knowing that he could not lose. Now he found his courage to be as flimsy and unreliable as his case.

"Why don't you put that thing away? All breakages must be paid for..." Gunner suggested as the hunter paced around the workshop, his hand-gun-hand drawn and glowing. Her tone was relaxed, but she made sure to keep Terry's attention ... to stop his eyes from straying too high. "How old is that case of yours?" she continued. "A year? I confess, if I keep a case for more than a week, I start to get twitchy. Why don't you relax and let Mr Coil show you some cases that are a little more 'today'..."

"I know you're here, Scrap! You and those stinks!"

the hunter cried, all but oblivious to Gunner and Coil. He reached into his cloak and pulled out an egg-shaped core. It was charred, scorched and glowed faintly in his hand. "See what you did? See what you did to my sister?"

Scrap knew the clock was ticking until they were discovered. His eyes darted around the web of wires for a way out. Ahead of Paige, where the web met the wall, square vents sucked hot air to the outside. Small, but large enough for a junk case and a pair of half-grown humans.

An escape route.

"That's your sister?" Gunner asked, below them. "What happened? She looks like she's in need of a new case, which means you've come to the right place…"

From the web, Scrap pointed Paige towards the vent. Paige nodded and, with Gnat clinging to her back, began edging across the wires. Scrap followed behind, so closely that the bottom of Paige's boots left dusty prints on his face.

"The only thing I need is to junk that junk case and collect my trophies," Terry replied, finally squaring up to Gunner. His voice became a mad howl. "There's no hiding from me, Scrap … no mistaking that *human stink*."

"Did you say 'human'?" gasped Gunner. Without meaning to, she glanced up.

The hunter's silvery sphere of a head rolled slowly backwards and peered into the web. In an instant he spotted Scrap, Paige and Gnat crawling across the wires towards the vent.

"*Gotcha*," grinned the hunter. With a swift kick, he sent Gunner flying backwards across the workshop, before aiming his hand-gun-hand up at the web. "You can hide, but you can't run!"

The blast flashed past Scrap's head, burning through metres of wires and a half-constructed case. Loose wires suddenly whipped around him as a portion of the webbing gave way. Paige leaped for the vent, diving through with Gnat still on her back. Scrap felt himself plummet, before his grappling claw shot out of his arm with a dry hiss, clasping the edge of the vent with a tinny clang. He swung hard into the wall as Terry took aim again.

"No!"

Corpus Coil's defiant cry was metal grinding against metal. In a blur of movement, the spidery robot reared up on his four back legs and pounced on the hunter, pinning him to the floor. Scrap would look back on the moment, quite sure that Coil was thinking not of him but of protecting his precious cases. Nevertheless, it gave him the seconds he needed to retract his grapple and flee inside the vent. He looked back and saw Gunner sprawled and dazed on the floor, and the hunter thrashing under Coil's steely grip. Scrap paused for a moment, until he heard Gnat's voice echo back up the vent. She was calling Scrap's name. He quickly followed her cries as more blasts rang out.

By the time Scrap scrambled out of the vent and fled into the encroaching gloom of evening with the humans, the fight was over. It had sounded quick, savage. Scrap hoped it had ended well for Gunner and the spidery Corpus Coil.

But only the hunter had walked away.

# IN THE SHADOWS

*It was in our programming to ask questions.*
*What can I do? How can I help? How can I serve?*
*But no one thought to ask the most important question of all:*
*Why should I?*

**From Memoir of a Mechanical Mayor by Harmony Highshine**

Scrap, Paige and Gnat raced through the city streets. They sought out every shadow they could, and avoided the revealing glow of every floating neon sign. In the end, they found their way to a narrow river, glowing an iridescent turquoise and filled with drone-fish. The three of them huddled under a bridge, tucking into the darkest shadow they could find, hidden even from the glow of the neon billboards.

Gnat pulled off her helmet, breathless and tearful. "I want to go home. I want to see Mum."

"I know," said Paige. She removed her own helmet cautiously, her eyes darting and wild. "Do you think they killed him? The hunter?"

"Robots don't junk robots," Scrap said. "But … I don't know. It was two against -zk- one. Maybe they beat him. Maybe they—"

Paige interrupted Scrap without looking at him.

"He'll keep coming, won't he?"

"Probably," Scrap replied. "He's -zk- got your scent."

And now the mayor was after them too, Scrap thought. Could she have learned who he was – who he used to be? If so, he was putting Paige and Gnat in danger just by being near them. And yet even if they went their separate ways, the hunter would surely still find them. Everything was going from bad to worse.

"We have to find the ship," Paige insisted. "We have to get off-world."

"I want Mum…" Gnat sobbed. "I'm hungry."

Paige rootled in her poncho and pulled out another green ball. "That's the last one," she said, taking the smallest of bites before handing it to her sister. She rubbed her eyes … ground her teeth. "We need to find food."

"There's food at home," Gnat said. "Mum will make

us soup."

"Gnat—"

"Well, she *will*," Gnat insisted, chomping away. "I hate plant balls. They taste like old granny feet."

"We can't go home. We need to find the ship first, you know that," Paige said, her voice shaking a little. She sounded less convinced than ever that their mission to find the *Pink-Footed Goose* was possible.

Gnat put her hand on Paige's arm. "We'll be OK. We've got Scrap."

Paige let out an exasperated grunt.

"If it wasn't for Scrap, we wouldn't even be in the city," she said, not looking at him. "We'd be on our way to the Elsewhere."

Scrap shook his head. "You still don't get it, do you? Your mission is -zk- idiotic. Gnat's right – you need to go *home*."

"And I told you, we can't!" Paige snapped.

Scrap flung up his arms. "For cog's sake, why?"

"Because we can't!" growled Paige. "You want to go back to your precious Pile, fine! But *we* are going to the Elsewhere."

"Fine, maybe I will!" shouted Scrap. "Maybe I'll try to -zk- rebuild the home you blew to -zk- bits!"

"Maybe you should!"

With that, Scrap and Paige seethed in angry silence.

"I hate when you two argue," said Gnat at last. "It's un-helping us and un-helping the mission and un-helping helping Mum."

A chided Scrap grunted, then he and Paige crossed their arms in huffy unison.

"You should say 'friends forever' and hug," suggested Gnat.

"Shut up, Gnat," tutted Paige.

"Shut up shutting me up," replied Gnat, happy with her comeback.

"Then stop saying stupid—"

Scrap shot out his arm, enough to stop Paige in her tracks. The trio lurched back into the shadows as the clanking footsteps and crackling voices echoed under the bridge.

Robots. Broad cube-haulers at least twice their size.

"...Cutter says he could've sold every seat in the Strongbox three times over," remarked one, striding obliviously towards the huddled trio. "You betting on tonight's bout?"

"Ten chunks of charge," another replied. "Victor Da Spoils is *unstoppable* this season."

As the robots passed by, Paige pushed her sister further back into the shadows, while Scrap craned to listen.

"You're betting ten chunks on the challenger?" the other cube-hauler said. "You could buy a new arm with that."

"When Da Spoils beats the champ, I'll pocket enough charge to upgrade my whole *case*," the robot said, "while you'll still be creaking around in that month-old rust bucket."

"Yeah, well – Morten Prometheus has been in the same case since the Difference of Opinion, and so far he's wiped the floor with every 'bot this side of the Elsewhere."

"Well, tonight's goin' to be different," concluded the first cube-hauler as they disappeared into the distance. "Mark my words, this is goin' to be a bout like no other…"

Scrap shook his head in the darkness. These "'Bot Bouts" sounded like nothing more than pointless punching, he thought. When he junked the cases of Somewhere 513's rebellious robots, he did so in the name of loyalty and liberty, boldly defending the humans against their cruel captors. His battles *meant* something. At least, he thought so at the time.

Now, he wished he'd never thrown the first punch.

A few dozen robots passed under the bridge, each theorizing about the outcome of the upcoming clash. When the coast finally appeared clear, Scrap turned to Paige and Gnat.

"Y'know, this could be our chance," he whispered. "With so many 'bots goin' to the -zk- fight, we might be able to get out of the city unnoticed."

"I thought you weren't leaving till you got an upgrade," huffed Paige.

"I never said – look, do you want to get out of here alive or -zk- not?" Scrap hissed, setting out in the opposite direction to the other robots. "Just stay in the shadows and stay out of sight, got that? Whatever happens, keep quiet and stay hid—"

A glancing blow to Scrap's shoulder sent him stumbling backwards. He turned to see a bright floating billboard pass almost overhead. It emitted an eerie neon glow, projecting a flickering image of two burly robots squaring off in hand-to-hand combat.

## 'BOT BOUTS – ROUND 15
## VICTOR DA SPOILS VS MORTEN PROMETHEUS

### THE STRONGBOX BOUT BEGINS IN 17:52

Scrap's jaw fell open, sending a loose screw clinking to the ground. He immediately leaped to his feet and pursued the billboard as it moved slowly under the bridge.

"Stay in the shadows and stay out of sight, got that!" whispered Gnat loudly.

Scrap didn't hear a word. He just gazed in horror at the robots on the billboard. "Morten Prometheus…?" he muttered. He didn't know the name, but he recognized the robot immediately.

In fact, it was like looking in a mirror.

# EPISODE 19

# THE STRONGBOX

```
      NAME  X  MORTEN PROMETHEUS
    HEIGHT  X  2.5 METRES
    WEIGHT  X  855KG
      CASE  X  SCRATCH-BUILT
SIGNATURE MOVE  X  FLYING SERVO-SLAM
     TAUNT  X  "Get your case out
               of Morten's Face"
```

"For cog's sake, that thievin' gub!"

Scrap stamped his foot so hard it rattled. As the billboard floated away under the bridge, he began spitting out expletives that Gnat was sure were so rude that she would never be allowed to say them.

"What is it? What's the matter?" Paige asked.

"He took it ... he -zk- took it!" barked Scrap. "The Strongbox ... I've got to get to the Strongbox..."

"The Strongbox?" Paige replied in an urgent whisper. "You just said we should stay out of sight and—"

"Change of plan!" Scrap interrupted. "Just -zk- stay here! I -zk- I'll come back for you…"

With that, he started making his way alongside the river as fast as Paige and Gnat had seen him move.

"But we want to stay with you!" Gnat shouted after him. "We want to stay with you, Scrap!"

Paige looked at Gnat, Gnat looked at Paige, in their sanctuary of shadows under the bridge.

Then, without saying a word, they replaced their helmets, and raced after Scrap.

## BOUT BEGINS IN 10:39

The sisters had a hard time keeping up with the diminutive, one-footed robot as he made his way through the city. He limped with a determination they'd not seen before, even when they were fleeing for their lives. The streets were narrow, with uneven, cube-built buildings rising up on both sides, and an increasing number of robots wandering here and there. Paige and Gnat ducked under legs, between wheels and around robots of every conceivable shape, size and design. Every minute or so, Scrap would stop to look up and, sure enough, a floating billboard or bright neon arrow would point in the direction of the Strongbox, accompanied by a countdown:

## BOUT BEGINS IN 05:08

Each direction only made Scrap redouble his efforts to reach his destination, and made keeping up with him even harder.

## BOUT BEGINS IN 02:14

A clamour of noise announced the Strongbox long before Scrap saw the huge cube, looming at the end of a busy, narrow street. The building seemed to be half buried, as red light emanated from an open doorway leading underground. Paige and Gnat were still fifty paces from Scrap when they saw him pushing past larger, finer robots with redoubled resolve, before hurrying through the doorway and disappearing inside.

Paige squeezed her sister's hand tightly, nerves and common sense getting the better of her. She looked down at her core tracer, its tiny screen confirming what she already knew – the Strongbox was teeming with robot life.

*Turn back*, she told herself, but with a river of jostling robots behind them, neither she nor Gnat had any chance of turning back or even slowing down. They were all but carried towards the glowing doorway and into the subterranean arena.

The noise hit them first. More noise than they had

ever heard – robot chatter echoed around the cube. What struck them next was a wall of heat and thick, metallic-tasting air. A long, wide ramp lead to another cube, standing in the centre of the room. Metal rods jutted vertically from each corner, with cables strung from one to the other. Paige already knew what this was – a fighting arena. A dozen or so hovering video-drones buzzed around it, waiting for the bout to begin, eager to record every moment.

As the last of the robots took their seats, Paige spotted a rotund, gaudily coloured robot hovering in the air several metres above the floor of the arena, its voice echoing to every corner of the Strongbox.

"*Mayor Highshine is proud to celebrate our rich cultural traditions through the time-honoured enjoyment of ritual skirmish! 'Bot versus 'bot! Power-driven prize fighters, proudly punching their way to victory and upgrades! I'm your host, Cal Cutter, and this is the night you've been waiting for … this is 'Bot Bouts, Round 15!*"

"UFff…!" Paige grunted as a passing robot bumped into her, knocking her on to the ramp.

"*In Rock 'Em corner,*" Cal Cutter continued, "*weighing in at 711 kilos … he may be chatty, but his actions speak louder than words, it's Victor Da Spoils!*"

The roar grew louder as a huge, egg-shaped robot with long, broad arms clambered into the ring.

"Where's Scrap?" asked Gnat. "I can't see Scrap…"

"*In Sock 'Em corner, weighing in at 855 kilos … don't be fooled 'cause he's old-school! He's the never-in-doubt King of the Bouts, it's Morten Prometheus!*"

Another roar. The blue and grey titan that stepped into the ring was by far the biggest robot in the building – two and a half metres of metal brawn. His entire body was covered in numerous scratches, dings and dents, which didn't seem to bother the metal giant one jot. A deep blue cape cascaded down his back, decorated with a bright star field – a map of some unknown galaxy.

"*One winner! No time limit! Knock out or tap out!*" The announcer bellowed. "*Seconds out, round one!*"

Without pause, Morten Prometheus thumped his opponent so hard that Victor Da Spoils was lifted off his feet. He collided with the taut metal ropes and fell backwards out of the arena, crashing to the ground inches from the front row of spectators.

"*Morten Prometheus comes out swinging! Victor Da Spoils is down and out of the arena!*" boomed the announcer. "*Looks like it's going to be another good day for the champion of the 'Bot Bouts!*"

"Hey!"

The cry was barely loud enough to register over the din, but Paige recognized the voice. She paused, and turned.

Another robot was climbing into the arena.

It was Scrap.

# MORTEN PROMETHEUS VS SCRAP

*If you are looking for answers, remember to keep your eyes open.*

**From Memoir of a Mechanical Mayor by Harmony Highshine**

T he Strongbox fell silent.

Paige and Gnat watched in bewildered horror as Scrap clambered clumsily under the arena's cables.

"What … is … he … *doing?*" Paige uttered under her breath.

"He's being King of the Robots…" Gnat whispered as the little robot limped his way to the centre of the arena.

"*What's this?*" cried the announcer. "*Another 'bot is entering the ring! He must have a screw loose! In fact, by the looks of him, he might have more than one. I've never seen a case like it!*"

"Oh, this is bad," said Paige over the hollering robots. "We need to get out of here, *now*."

"We can't go," Gnat protested. "Scrap's doing a big 'bot fight with a big 'Bot Bouts 'bot…"

"He can look after himself!" Paige snapped, trying to pull her sister back up the ramp. "And even if he can't, there's nothing we can do about it…"

"Scrap!" Gnat cried, but Scrap did not hear her. His singular focus was the robot known as Morten Prometheus. He limped boldly towards the metal titan who peered curiously down at him.

"That's not yours," Scrap said. He squared up to Morten Prometheus's right knee and craned his neck to look up at him, fists clenched and shaking.

"What's this, a tag-team bout?" groaned a dazed Victor Da Spoils, clambering back up into the arena. "Who's your little friend, Prometheus?"

"Morten Prometheus has no friends, only challengers," boomed the robot grandly. Then he leaned down towards Scrap and pointed a great thumb towards the entrance. "Are you lost, junk case? The Piles are that way…"

Laughter rose up from the crowd, but Scrap did not

take his eyes off Morten Prometheus. "I said, that's not -zk- yours," he repeated, his voice louder, angrier. He was shaking so hard that rust flaked from his case.

"You should go back to your seat – Morten Prometheus does not want to tread on you," suggested Morten, and the crowd laughed again. With a roar, Scrap reached back his leg (the one with the foot) and kicked the giant robot in the shin as hard as he could. Though Morten barely felt it, the effort sent Scrap tumbling back on to the floor.

"*Looks like this junk case has a death wish!*" Cal Cutter declared from above the arena. "*He's going to need an upgrade or ten to go toe to toe with the big 'bots! I hope Morten Prometheus is in a forgiving mood…*"

"New sparring partner, Prometheus?" mocked Victor Da Spoils, watching Scrap scramble to his feet.

"Not yours!" Scrap shouted again.

"What is not Morten's?" Morten asked. "What is your malfunction, junk case?"

"I'm functionin' just -zk- fine," snapped Scrap, his right kneecap falling off with inconvenient timing. He clamped it back on and then pointed at Morten with an outstretched arm. "Well enough to know that's -zk- *not your case*."

"Morten's … case? What are you talking about?"

asked Morten uneasily.

"You know!" Scrap snarled, rage twisting in the pit of his core. "You know what I'm -zk- talkin' about!"

"You've got a screw loose, junk case – and not 'cause I can literally see one hanging out of your head," thundered Victor Da Spoils. "Morten Prometheus *built* that case himself – everybody knows that. He was the first 'bot on Five One Three to upgrade!" He reached down, plucked Scrap up by the scruff of his neck, and held him in front of his face. "Now why don't you hop it before someone gets—"

Victor did not see Scrap's leg coming – the footless stump jabbed him hard in the eye. Victor squealed in surprise, dropping Scrap as he lurched backwards and tumbled out of the arena for a second time.

For a moment, nobody could believe what they had just seen. Even Paige and Gnat stopped struggling with each other for long enough to stare open-mouthed at the sight of Scrap sending a robot ten times his size sprawling.

Then the crowd went wild.

"Yeah!" Gnat cried with glee. "Go, Scrap! Kick off their heads!"

The sisters watched Scrap pull himself to his feet

again and call out in rage.

"Admit that's not your case!" he howled at Morten Prometheus.

"M-Morten Prometheus does not know what you are talking about," Morten replied, sounding increasingly less assured. He rolled his shoulders and Scrap heard the whirr of his motors. "Now come on, junk case, you look like you are on your last legs, and also one of your legs does not even have a foot. Morten does not want to hurt you, so why not just—"

Scrap roared, racing towards the metal colossus and clambering up his leg. Before Morten Prometheus could grab him, Scrap had managed to climb up on to his back.

"Stop that – get off!" Morten Prometheus insisted. It took a simple flex of his shoulder to fling the little junk case through the air. Scrap instinctively reached out his left arm – with a *Pffff!* his clawed hand shot out of his wrist on a cable and clamped on to the giant robot's face. Morten Prometheus shrieked in horror and began lurching around the arena. He floundered into the ropes and fell backwards, crashing on to his back. Scrap, still clamped to the giant's face, was dragged through the air before landing squarely on the giant's chest. He immediately began pounding it with his spare hand.

"Not ... your ... case!" he screamed. As Victor Da Spoils crawled back into the arena for a second time, a panicking Morten Prometheus wrenched Scrap's claw from his face and spun the cable in the air like a lasso. Scrap whirled through the air, jabbing Victor Da Spoils in the eye again as he did so, and sending him toppling back into the crowd.

"Off!" Morten Prometheus screamed, and with one final swing he tossed Scrap roughly on to the floor of the arena.

"Scraaap!" Gnat screamed as more cheers rang out from the crowd. She pulled hard and freed herself from Paige's grip. By the time Paige realized her hand was empty, Gnat was racing towards the ring. Paige screamed her sister's name, just in time to see Gnat trip, and trip again, and fall. Within an instant she was rolling uncontrollably down the ramp, tumbling past rows of robots seated on cube-shaped seats. Finally she collided with the base of the arena with a bone-rattling thud.

"GNAT!"

As her sister raced down the ramp towards her, Gnat sat up and felt a bruise already forming on the back of her head. Then it dawned on her that, with her disguise in place, she shouldn't be able to rub the back of her head at all.

She reached both hands up to her face and patted the soft skin with her fingers.

She wasn't wearing her helmet.

Gnat had lost her head.

"Oops..." she muttered. An instant later, Paige barrelled into her. She pulled her own helmet from her head and, for a horrified moment, the pair stared into each other's wide and fearful eyes, before Paige slammed her helmet roughly over her sister's head. As Gnat let out a muffled "Pai-mmph!" Paige pulled up the hood of her poncho. She glanced around to see if anyone had noticed what had happened, but it seemed as though Scrap's sudden appearance was keeping all eyes firmly fixed on the arena.

"Come on!" Paige ordered as she yanked her sister to her feet.

"What about Scrap?" cried Gnat. Paige pulled her hood further over her face – she had already decided there was nothing she could do to help the little robot and, all things considered, they were better off without him.

"Forget him!" she hissed as Gnat found more strength to struggle.

"No! Scrap!" she screamed, reaching out for the arena with one arm as Paige tried to pull her away by the other.

Scrap did not hear her cries. He was sprawled out on the ground, his head spinning. He tried to get to his feet, but barely managed to drag himself along the floor as Morten Prometheus's great shadow fell over him. He rolled on to his back as the champion of the 'Bot Bouts raised his right leg. With his brain-frame rattling in his head, Scrap focused on the bottom of the robot's foot. He stared at it as if inspecting a crime scene.

"I -zk- knew it!" he cried, his voice hoarse with defiance. "Not your -zk- case! That's not your—"

"Be quiet!" hissed Morten Prometheus.

Then, as Gnat screamed again, he stamped on Scrap with all his might.

# INTERLUDE TWO

## TWO MINUTES EARLIER

Harmony Highshine leaned back in her chair. A dozen screens sent light flickering across her face. She hadn't left the Ivory Tower in months, but the myriad video-drones that floated around the city fed her up-to-the-second footage and made sure she kept her eye on proceedings. The 'Bot Bouts were a particular highlight. She made sure her drones recorded each moment and every corner of the bouts. Once a week, she would take a break from the twin vexations of upgrading and evolution and enjoy watching two robots pummel each other senseless.

But this wasn't part of the show.

"*What's this? Another 'bot is entering the ring! He must have a screw loose! In fact, by the looks of him, he might have more than one. I've never seen a case like it!*"

The announcer sounded as surprised as the crowd, which rumbled in confusion. Highshine gazed at the screens one by one. Each screen relayed the 'Bot Bouts' strange interruption from a different angle. A tiny robot was clambering awkwardly into the ring.

"*You…!*" Highshine whispered. "How'd you give Gunner the slip?"

"Madame Mayor?"

Highshine had not noticed the door open. Her outer shell closed around her in an instant.

"Do I need to get a sign, Domo?" she said, not taking her eyes off the screens.

"…Madame Mayor?"

"For the door. I was thinking something easy to interpret like, 'please knock'."

Domo began wheeling back out of the doorway.

"So sorry, Madame Mayor, I shall—"

"*Please* don't go out and come in again," the mayor said, her eyes fixed on the central screen as Scrap squared up to Morten Prometheus. "We just need to keep this new me under wraps. The robots of Somewhere Five One Three are not yet ready to accept this next phase."

"I couldn't agree more," said Domo. "Honestly, I find it a little confusing myself."

"It's a matter of evolution, Domo," said Highshine. She finally turned to face him. "You *do* want me to evolve, don't you, Domo?"

Domo spoke without hesitation. "Whatever it takes."

"Glad to hear it," said the mayor, turning back to

the screens. "Now I assume you're here to tell me that Gunner has failed to keep a tendril-hold on the-'bot-who-would-be-King?"

"I – how did you know?"

"Robot's intuition. What happened?"

"You're quite correct," Domo replied. "I'm afraid there has been an *incident* at the emporium."

"Incident?" repeated Highshine.

"An outlier from the east – a hunter identified as T3-RY appeared on the scene in search of the three junk cases of interest."

"A hunter? The plot thickens. What happened?"

"There was a tussle. Sheriff Niner has confirmed that K11-LU and C0-IL have been … reduced in functionality."

"Say 'junked' if you mean junked, Domo," huffed the mayor. On the screens, she watched Scrap doing battle with Morten Prometheus. "Gunner and Coil, are they all right?"

"Both need their cases replacing. They've been taken to the city sick bay to have their cores checked. But as you say, I'm afraid K1-NG got away."

"King? Oh, I know exactly where he is," said Highshine, tapping the display's central screen with her finger. "There."

"I don't understand…" said Domo, peering at the screen. Sure enough, there was a junk case squaring fearlessly up to the mighty Morten Prometheus. "*Him?*" Domo added, almost laughing. "You really think that's K1-NG?"

"I don't know any other 'bot with the core to pick a fight with the champion of the 'Bot Bouts, do you?" Highshine replied, tapping the screen with a silver finger. "What I don't know is what he's doing in my city. I like to think everything happens for a reason, Domo, but so far King's sudden reappearance is quite the … most … baffling…"

Highshine had spotted a commotion in the audience. She spun towards the screen in the bottom left of her array, practically shoving her deputy out of the way. She stared at the screen in the way that Domo longed for the mayor to look at him – with sheer, undiluted awe.

"Madame Mayor…?" he uttered after an awkward pause.

"Did you see that?" Highshine gasped. "*Did you see that?* Domo, get on the playback. Rewind camera eight…"

Domo hurried to the video controls and began

spooling the data backwards.

"No, not the ring – the *crowd*. Camera eight – no, nine! Camera nine," the mayor said, her eyes darting from screen to screen. "Back further … further … wait, there. *There*. Freeze the frame!"

"What … what am I looking at, Madame Mayor?" asked Domo, squinting to examine the image.

"You are looking at the *impossible*," she whispered.

Mayor Highshine leaned in, her arm passing over his shoulder, and pressed the screen in the bottom-left corner. In its centre was an image of two small, dazed-looking figures at the base of the arena, staring at each other. Though the image was grainy and juddering, both Domo and the mayor knew what they were looking at.

Humans.

"It can't be…" Domo gasped.

"It is…" whispered Highshine, leaning closer to the screen. "It *is*."

"How?" uttered Domo. "Could humans have returned to Somewhere Five One Three without us knowing?"

"Impossible – long-range sensors would have picked up any ships in the upper atmosphere. There's no way they … could … have…" The mayor trailed off and pressed her hand to her mouth. She leaned closer to the screen, her face almost touching it, and stared, wide-eyed at the quivering image.

"But it doesn't make sense…" Domo uttered, rolling nervously around the room, oblivious to the mayor's epiphany. "We saw the colonists leave – we *saw* the *Black-Necked Stork* blast off into the vast unknown. No human has set foot on this planet in ten years! It must be some mistake – a glitch in the feed. I'll have the video-drones recalled for servicing and examine the—"

"They're hers," interrupted Highshine.

"Madame Mayor…?"

"*They're hers*," she said again, tapping the screen with a finger. "Look – *look at them*, Domo. The resemblance is uncanny. They're hers … her children."

"They're children? It's hard to tell…" Domo inspected the screen again. "But whose?"

"Who else? Dandelion Brightside."

The mayor spoke the name slowly, almost reverently.

"The *maker*?" blurted Domo, unable to stifle a disbelieving laugh. "The maker is gone! She left with the others."

"Did she?" Highshine leaned back in her chair. "We saw their ship leave … but what if not everyone was on it? What if they stayed? What if … what if they've been here this whole time? And what if they *multiplied*?"

Highshine returned to the live feed. One of the humans had attempted to disguise themselves with what looked like a robot head. The other pulled up the hood of her poncho but none of the crowd seemed to notice them – they were too busy watching the little robot in the arena doing battle with Morten Prometheus.

"What does it all mean, Madame Mayor?" Domo asked, no less fretful for this new revelation. "First K1-NG, now the offspring of the maker? There must be some connection! Do – do you think they're in league? What could they be planning?"

Highshine watched Morten Prometheus slam his foot down upon Scrap with all his mechanical might. "If they do have a plan, it doesn't seem to be going well," she noted, and then looked back at the humans. "Either way, this changes *everything*. Whatever King hoped to achieve by coming here, he has inadvertently shown me the future."

"…Future?" Domo repeated.

"Evolution, Domo – the answer I've been looking for," whispered Harmony Highshine. "I think it's time we met our visitors, don't you?"

"If you say so, Madame Mayor," Domo replied. "Should I radio to the sheriff?"

Mayor Highshine shook her head. "Niner will go in all guns blazing – and he'll take all day to do it. No, we must move quietly, and quickly." With that, she tapped a metal finger against the central screen. "Get me my champion," she said. "Get me M0-TN."

# UNDERFOOT

*Long ago, before hundreds of Somewheres dotted the galaxy, human explorers would travel to distant lands not through the stars, but across oceans. Sometimes these water ships would be struck by storms, and sink to the bottom of the ocean. The captain would wait until every member of their crew was on a lifeboat before they left. Sometimes that meant they went down with their ship. Such was the fate of Dandelion Brightside.*

**From Memoir of a Mechanical Mayor *by Harmony Highshine***

S crap's torso buckled underfoot.

As Morten Prometheus pressed his foot down upon his chest, Scrap heard the rough *GRAWNCH* of crushing metal. As his systems failed once again, he felt his brain-frame sparking wildly, sending memories cascading through his mind.

Her. Of course it was her. It was always her.

Dandelion Brightside.

*If this is to be my last memory*, he thought, *let it be of the day I was first brought online ... the day*

*I first met Dandelion.*

*But it was another memory that insisted itself upon Scrap's fading brain-frame.*

*Not birth, but rebirth.*

*"There's my King," a voice said softly. "I knew you'd come back to me."*

*King opened his eyes to find her looking back at him. Dandelion Brightside. The only face he ever wanted to see.*

*This felt right. Everything felt right when he was with Dandelion.*

*"Hey, look who's alive!" said Tripp Gander. He leaned into view, looking pale and spent and strange. "How are you feeling, King?"*

*"...Different," he said. His voice was a raspy whirr and his limbs felt sluggish, dry and tired. "How'd I -zk- get away? Memory's fuzzy ... feels like my brain-frame can't keep up with my -zk- core..."*

*"Those K11s gave you quite a hiding," said Tripp, glancing uneasily at Dandelion.*

*"They're not so tough," King groaned. "There's not a 'bot on this Somewhere who's stronger than -zk- me."*

*"Same old King," said Dandelion with a sad smile as she*

and Tripp helped him to sit up. "Don't strain your servos. You're going to feel different for a while."

"Everything's going to feel different," Tripp added with a sigh.

"At least the plan -zk- worked," King said. "The K11s took the bait and cornered me in the town square. Those gubs did a number on me — I thought for a minute they might even junk my case. But I bought you enough -zk- time to get to the ship and get … away … from… Wait."

"King, listen to me—" Dandelion began.

"This isn't right … this isn't -zk- right," Scrap said, rapping on the side of his head to try and clear it. "What are you two -zk- doing here? What is this? Where am I?"

With gears grating, King looked around at the wide bunker lit from above by long fluorescent strips and packed with crates of equipment. Tools … supplies … rations … weapons … even a small moon-buggy.

"King—" Dandelion began.

"Is this a Foxhole?" King gasped. "For cog's— What are we -zk- doing … you're supposed to be on the ship … you were supposed to go with the others … you were supposed to leave."

"Somebody had to operate the launch pad," explained Dandelion. "Somebody had to get the Black-Necked Stork *off the ground – to get the colonists off-world."*

"We would have got a robot to do it," added Tripp. "But, y'know, they took our world from us."

"No … no -zk- no," King protested. "You said – you promised *you'd leave! I walked into a trap for you* so you could get away!"

"I know you did – and I also know you wouldn't have let us strand ourselves on Somewhere Five One Three," Dandelion said. "I'm sorry, King, but there was no other way. We had to make sure everyone else could leave."

"And at least we came back for you," added Tripp. "They had your case under lock and key in the town hall. We put our necks on the line sneaking back into the city to steal back your core. We risked our lives for you."

"Tripp…" said Dandelion.

"Well, we did," Tripp huffed. "You – we – risked everything going back for him."

"Be -zk- be -zk-…" King stuttered. "…Betrayed me…"

"Hey, mind your motors, King," snapped Tripp. "We saved *you.*"

"Betrayed me…" *King snarled again, struggling weakly to his feet, his limbs fizzing and sputtering.* "Promised you'd leave … promised you'd get -zk- off -zk- … cog's sake, what's -zk- wrong with my -zk- voice?"

"I'm sorry, King — it was hard enough getting your core out of your case with nothing but a shift-widget," Dandelion said, holding up what looked like a long, four-pronged screwdriver. "We barely got out of there without being discovered ... there was no way to save your case."

King stumbled, his legs all but giving out under him. "What did you -zk- do?" he said, tottering towards the nearby moon-buggy. "What did you -zk- do?"

King staggered into the buggy and steadied himself. He looked down at his hands, pressed against the bonnet. He didn't recognize them. They were tiny ... useless ... creaking and cracking with rust. He looked up and spotted a reflection in the windscreen. For the longest moment, he didn't believe it was him. It couldn't be him, this strange, ugly thing. Small, frail, slight, and built from mismatched pieces of metal that should have been consigned to the furnace years ago.

"It was the best I could do with what we had," said Dandelion as the robot gazed down in miserable horror at his case. "It — it's only temporary. I'll try to build you a better—"

"What did you do to me?" King howled.

"You could at least try not to be totally ungrateful," Tripp snapped. "Dandelion saved you. Without her you'd *be nothing but a core."*

*"Better that -zk- than this!" King screamed. "Better nothing than this! Better nothin' than King of the -zk- Junk Cases!"*

*King lurched away, staggering backwards before pivoting awkwardly towards the bunker's entrance. He spotted the narrow ladder leading up to the entrance hatch.*

*"King, wait!" Dandelion called after him. "We just need to wait until help comes... When we get out of here, I promise I'll make you better! Please, please don't go..."*

*"You made me. Designed me ... built me ... made me everything I am. Now you've turned me into nothing!" King roared. "I wouldn't stay here if you were the last humans on Somewhere! Which you -zk- are!"*

*He had never found something as simple as climbing a ladder so challenging. But with rage in his core, he dragged himself up every rung, Dandelion calling after him, and pressed the hatch release. With the loud detaching of turbo-locks and the grinding of gears, the hatch swung open. King closed his eyes as daylight poured in ... and he heard a voice in the distance cry out:*

*"Stop!"*

*Was it Dandelion?*

*"Stop it!"*

*No, it was someone else.*

*"Leave him alone!"*

*Gnat. It was Gnat's voice.*

*Suddenly, he remembered.*

*He was in the arena.*

She's here, *he thought.* Gnat's in the Strongbox.

And with that, Scrap woke up.

# KING OF THE ROBOTS

*I watched the humans escape Somewhere 513 – watched them blast off into space in their rocket ship. There were those robots who thought that was the end of our world. They knew that when the colonists told the corporation what we had done, our robotic revolution would simply be seen as a mass malfunction. Humankind would destroy us.*

*But they had no idea how far I would go to protect our world.*

**From Memoir of a Mechanical Mayor *by Harmony Highshine***

"**L**eave him alone!"

The first thing Scrap noticed was that he was awake, which was also when he realized that, somehow, he was still functioning. His core – his remarkable core had brought him back from the brink all on its own.

"Get off him!"

Amidst the clamour and chaos, Scrap could hear Gnat's voice echoing under her disguise, and realized that the humans had followed him into the Strongbox. He was still lying on his back with Morten Prometheus's foot – a foot almost as large as his entire case – pressing hard against his chest. He rolled his head to the left and saw – Paige? – no, Gnat wearing Paige's helmet. She was desperately trying to clamber into the arena. Behind her he saw Paige, one hand tugging down her hood over her head, the other trying to heave Gnat away.

"Leave him alone!" Gnat screamed again. "He's King of the Robots!"

The sound of that name was enough to make Morten Prometheus lift his foot off Scrap's chest. He all but stumbled backwards.

Scrap, meanwhile, barely gave his mangled torso a second's thought. Nothing could match the horror of hearing Gnat's words echo through the arena.

*She told them*, thought Scrap, cold with horror. *She told them who I am.*

The silence was like nothing Scrap had ever experienced. Even on the loneliest night on the Pile, the wind still whipped among the debris ... distant creatures still howled in the darkness. This was a total absence of sound, as hundreds of robots stared at him aghast. His core ran cold. With his torso all but flattened, he dragged himself awkwardly to a sitting position and opened his mouth to speak, but without the first clue as to whether he should admit who he was, deny everything or reveal the human's secret to protect his own, no words came.

That was when the laughter began.

Victor Da Spoils laughed first. The noise gurgled out of his mouth without warning. The crowd followed, one after the other, guffaws of disbelief, which quickly filled every corner of the arena.

*They don't believe it*, he thought. *Of course they don't believe it.*

Shame and rage engulfed him. He pulled himself awkwardly to his feet. He had lost a panel from his shoulder when he was thrown to the floor, so his right arm now hung loosely in its socket, and his chest was concave and sparking from where Morten Prometheus had stepped on him, but his core – his incredible core – was undamaged. Scrap managed to limp across the arena and topple clumsily on to the ramp. By now the laughter was deafening, and it consumed him. He didn't notice the floating video-drones quietly follow him up the ramp. He didn't see Morten Prometheus sidle to a corner of the arena to answer a call on his wrist radio. He didn't spot Gnat's helmet on the ground as he kicked it out of his path. He didn't even hear Gnat cry his name as he pushed past her, tripped twice, and stumbled out into the street.

It had started to rain. Scrap had always hated the rain on Somewhere 513 – it was oily and silver green and fell in angry, pummelling drops, each one as determined to batter, drench or rust his case as the next. As it hammered on the ground, the sound mingled with the laughter of the crowd, which still poured out of the entrance, raucous and giddy.

"Cog's sake…"

Scrap stumbled into a nearby alleyway, out of the red glare of the Strongbox, and fell to his knees. He should have been relieved. The last thing he wanted was to feel the same shame that had led him to banish himself to the Piles all those years ago. But the crowd's disbelief somehow felt worse. No one could even begin to believe that this lowly junk case had once been the best of them.

"Scrap…?"

Gnat's voice. Of *course* the humans had followed him. Paige and Gnat were a sorrier sight than ever. Though Paige had managed to grab her sister's helmet from the ramp, her attempt to squeeze it on to her own head left her looking like a wonky-faced, robot-human hybrid, while Gnat's oversized disguise made her head loll to one side.

"Just -zk- leave me be," he said, almost to himself.

Paige and Gnat turned to each other. They took off their helmets and quickly swapped, before pulling their ponchos tight around them as the rain did its worst to knock them off their feet. A moment later, they were at Scrap's side, helping him to his feet.

"Are you OK? You're all flat," said Gnat. She held up the panel that belonged to his right shoulder. "Also, this bit of you fell off but I got it."

"I -zk- said leave me -zk- alone…" Scrap uttered, his reply sounding nowhere near as commanding as he'd hoped.

"What happened back there?" Paige asked. "That robot – did you know him?"

"Not him…" Scrap sighed. Shimmering greenish raindrops pooled in puddles on the ground, reflecting his face back at him. "I knew his case."

"His case?" Paige repeated.

"He's changed it, added some -zk- parts … but there's no mistakin' that case – I'd -zk- know it anywhere," Scrap said. "It was *mine*."

"What are you talking about?" asked Paige, her voice almost lost to the thundering rain.

"He took my case!" Scrap howled, still holding his loose shoulder in its socket. "I don't know how, but 'Morten Prometheus' has got my case ... my *first* case."

Paige took a step back. She held her breath, letting his words sink in.

"You *are* him, aren't you?" she said at last. "King of the Robots."

"I reckon you knew that already ... just -zk- didn't want to believe it," sighed Scrap. "Your mum led you right to me."

Paige looked down at the screen on her core tracer, still pulsing brightly with his signal.

"Yeah," she muttered to herself. "I guess she did."

"Excuse me, I knew it too," Gnat said, jabbing Paige with her elbow. "I told you who he was for this whole time."

Paige smiled under her helmet.

"Yeah, you did," she muttered. "Clever cub."

Scrap stood up slowly and turned to face the humans.

"My core-code – my *name* was K1-NG," he said. "It was your dad who named me 'King of the Robots', for all the -zk- good it did me."

"You should have told us," Paige said, glowering at Scrap. "Why didn't you just *tell* us when we found you?"

"Would it have -zk- made any -zk- difference?" asked Scrap.

"Of course it would!" Paige protested. "You had a million chances to tell us! If I'd have known, then—"

"Then what? What did it matter either way? The moment you turned up at my door, my -zk- life was ruined all over again," snapped Scrap, jabbing his chest with his thumb. "Why would she — why would your mum send you to find me? She knew I was like this. She *made* me like this. She must've been out of her mind to think I could help you."

Paige clenched her fists. "Don't you talk about Mum..."

"Dandelion Brightside made everythin' that makes me, me," said Scrap defensively. "She designed me ... built my case ... fitted my core with her -zk- own two hands. She's your mother, but she might as well be my mother too."

Gnat let out a squeal. "Paaaaaaige, we're sister and brother with Scrap," she said, her mind blown. "We're sister and brother and sister!"

"Oh, and she ruined my life," Scrap added, throwing out his arms. "Some -zk- mother..."

Scrap barely saw Paige coming before she planted

both palms on his chest and shoved him so hard he was lifted into the air. In an instant he was sprawled on the ground again.

"You shut up about Mum!" Paige growled, clenching her fists. She stood over Scrap, face red and knuckles white. "You don't get to say anything about her! You don't get to pretend she's— You're a robot! You weren't born, you were built. You think you're real, but we made you. You're just a – a thing!"

Scrap went to speak, but nothing came out but a sad, tinny wheeze. He noticed his kneecap was hanging loose. He tried to push it back into place, before spotting a handful of nuts and screws had dislodged in his fall and lay scattered around him in the puddles. Scrap sighed again and slowly started fishing them out of the water.

"He's not a thing, he's King of the Robots, and he's called Scrap," Gnat said, helping to pick up his pieces with him. "And he's poorly, so don't be horrid to him."

Paige's frustrated growl was swallowed up by the sound of the downpour. She stamped her feet once, twice, in the rain. Then her rage and strength seemed to leave her in a single breath.

A moment later, Paige knelt in the pooling water and collected up the last of Scrap's parts.

# ONE ROBOT AGAINST A THOUSAND

*Thinking of going Somewhere?*
*At the Fargone Corporation, we're so confident that*
*you'll love your new Somewhere, that if you're not 100% satisfied,*
*we'll pay your return fare ourselves.*

*Because when you go Somewhere, you'll never want to come home.*

**From Your Guide to a New Somewhere**
**By the Fargone Corporation**

After Paige and Gnat collected Scrap's loose parts into Paige's satchel, the trio moved further into the gloom of the alleyway, away from the glow and rumble of the Strongbox.

Above them, a wide walkway between the buildings offered shelter from the rain. They huddled in the darkness, listening to the cascading drops batter the city. Then Gnat jabbed her sister in the ribs.

"What? Ugh, fine…" Paige murmured. Then, without turning to Scrap, she said, "Sorry I pushed you."

"Yeah," said Scrap. He popped his shoulder back into its socket. "I'm gettin' used to bein' -zk- pushed around."

"Mum said you always stood up for what you believed in," said Gnat. "She said you fighted every robot in the whole Somewhere to save them."

"Fought," Paige corrected her. She turned to Scrap. "Is it true? Did you fight them all?"

For a few moments, Scrap watched the rainfall in silence. "It's a story I've tried to forget," he said after a while. "I was the only robot on the *Black-Necked Stork*. I hardly even knew any other 'bots. I guess I wasn't sure what to expect, but not a -zk- *revolution*."

"What's a 'reddy-looshun'?" asked Gnat. Paige shushed her again.

"By the time we got to Five One Three, the 'bots had made their -zk- minds up," Scrap continued. "It was the K11s who did the talkin' – they told us they didn't want to hand over the planet, sayin' they wanted to be free, whatever that meant. They'd decided they -zk- deserved Somewhere Five One Three. I didn't know where it had all come from … rusted brain-frames or crossed wires. I s'pose I just didn't think the 'bots would really put up a fight against K1-NG, but they did. And do you know what? That was -zk- fine. That was *great*. I was right there in the thick of it, one robot against a thousand. I thought I could put them in their place. I -zk- thought I could teach 'em a lesson."

"Is that why you fought?" Paige asked. "To teach them a lesson?"

"I mean, I wasn't about to let 'em kick the humans off their own world, but yeah, I guess I thought I could knock some -zk- sense into 'em," Scrap replied. "Thing I don't understand is why no one came lookin' for your parents. Not the colonists, not the Corporation ... your -zk- folks helped the colonists get away, an' for their troubles everyone seemed to forget all about 'em ... an' you gubs had to spend your whole lives as -zk- mole-people."

"I'm a mole-people!" Gnat happily affirmed.

"I guess I fought for the humans 'cause I was the only one who -zk- could," Scrap added. "And 'cause I didn't think I'd lose."

"But you *did* lose," Paige said coolly.

"Of *course* I lost. One robot against a -zk- thousand? How could it turn out any other way?" Scrap cried. "I thought one 'bot could take on the world. I should have known better."

"Mum says you even fighted at the end, so the peoples

had time to get away," said Gnat proudly.

"Did she tell you she -zk- lied to me?" grunted Scrap. "I walked into a trap so your mum and dad could escape this cog-forsaken rock, but they stayed. I felt ... betrayed. Plus your mum -zk- doomed me with this sorry excuse for a case, presumably just so that, ten years later, her kids could make my life a -zk- misery."

"He's talking about us," Gnat informed Paige helpfully.

"An' you know what? She lied to you too," added Scrap. "King of the Robots, am I? You -zk- saw what happened back in the arena. Nobody believed I was K1-NG – they took one look at me and laughed. This is my punishment for helpin' the humans – a lifetime as the lowest of the -zk- low, stuck in this good-for-nothin' junk case for the rest of my good-for-nothin' days. That's what I got for pickin' the wrong side. No -zk- offence."

Gnat sniffed.

"You're still going to help us though, right? You're going to help us find the ship and rescue Mum?"

Paige let out a strange, stifled groan as she pushed a hundred terrible feelings back down into the pit of her gut.

"Let him be, Gnat," she said. "You heard him. He can't

help us."

The three of them sat for a few moments, watching the rain start to ease.

"Yesterday, on the train," said Scrap, breaking the silence, "you asked me if I could turn my dreams off."

"Yeah?" Paige said as a question.

"I leave 'em on 'cause, if I'm lucky, I dream of bein' him ... of being K1-NG again," he explained. "I leave 'em on 'cause then I stand a chance of bein' someone other than -zk- me for a while."

"If you hate that case so much, why didn't you let them upgrade you?" Paige asked. "Why didn't you let Gunner shift your core into a new body?"

"I couldn't upgrade without givin' them my core-code, could I?" Scrap replied. "If they'd found out I was K1-NG ... well, you heard what Gunner said – Second Suggestion or no Second Suggestion, she would've -zk- *killed* me. And if not her, then someone else. Back in the war, I junked dozens of cases, fightin' for the humans. We're in enough trouble with that hunter, without the whole -zk- city turnin' on us. So I'm stuck like this. I can't upgrade, not ever. Which means I'm no -zk- good to anyone. Not you, not your sister, and not your mum."

Paige looked away. "I could do it."

"Do what?" Scrap asked.

"Shift your core. Mum showed me how."

Scrap's laugh escaped like a cough. Paige glowered at him.

"Wait, you mean it?" Scrap gasped. "You're -zk- serious?"

"Mum taught me about robots every day. It was all there was to do. I've learned design … programming … repairs … and upgrading," Paige said. "If we had a case to put you in, yeah, I reckon I could upgrade you."

Scrap rubbed his temples for a long moment. "An' you didn't -zk- think to mention this earlier?" he howled.

"You didn't think to tell me you were King of the Robots," Paige snapped back.

"That's not the … that's a totally different … I could have … argh!" Scrap's scream echoed through the alleyway. "There were a -zk- thousand empty cases on the Pile! Any one of them would've been -zk- better than this! Now we're stuck in the middle of the city with no charge! Where on Somewhere are we going to get hold of—"

Suddenly Scrap saw stars. A galaxy flashed before his eyes in the sweep of a cape. An instant later he, Paige and Gnat were engulfed in darkness.

# AT HOME WITH MORTEN PROMETHEUS

Give your 'bot a boost with the

**MORE POWER TO YOU™**
**HIGH-SPEED CORE BATTERY**

No more searching for a charge station – simply rapid-charge
your robot's core from the comfort of your own home.

**MORE POWER TO YOU™**

Power to your robot, Power to you.

Scrap wasn't sure how long he and the humans had spent bundled and buffeted in blackness as they were transported who-knows-where.

It was long enough for him to wonder what terrible fate awaited them, but not quite long enough to work out how to escape. The one thing Scrap did establish was exactly where they were. The faint glow from his left eye illuminated the inside of their cloth prison just enough for him to make out the myriad shapes decorating it.

A star field. They were inside Morten Prometheus's cape.

"Morten is going to let you out now," a voice whispered at last. "Please do not shoot your hand into Morten's face..."

Scrap was about to give Morten Prometheus a piece of his mind, when he saw a blinking red light appear in the darkness.

Paige had found her grenade.

"For cog's— Would you *stop* tryin' to blow us up?" Scrap snapped. An instant later, all three of them tumbled on to a well-polished floor. Morten Prometheus towered in front of them, drenched in rain.

"Morten agrees – *please* do not blow us up," declared Morten Prometheus. He dropped his cape on the floor and raised his huge arms in the air, as if in surrender, adding, "Morten is not good with violence."

"Ha!" scoffed Scrap, resting his hand on his flattened chest panel. "That's rich, comin' from a prize fighter."

"That is *theatre*," replied Morten Prometheus. He watched Paige disarm her grenade before returning it to her satchel, and breathed a loud sigh of relief. "Morten batters 'bots in the Strongbox, but it is all for show – it is *pretend*."

"You'd know all about -zk- pretendin', wouldn't you?" sneered Scrap. He jabbed at his flattened torso. "What's the big idea, kidnappin' us? Haven't you done enough damage?"

"Morten is very sorry about slightly abducting you," explained the enormous robot. "Morten did not know how else to get you here … and did not want to leave you like *that*."

Scrap clenched his fists as Morten reached out towards Scrap with both hands. He yelped as the great robot grasped his torso. With the now familiar sound of buckling metal, Morten effortlessly bent Scrap's body back into shape.

"There," added Morten, with an apologetic smile. "That is better."

"Better than -zk- junked maybe," Scrap huffed. "Not exactly what I'd call an upgrade though…"

"Sorry also about somewhat treading on you – Morten panicked because you knew about this case," Morten said, holding his hand to his chest. "Who are you?"

"I'm Gnat-Bot Ninety-Nine and that's Paige and that's Scrap," Gnat loudly interjected.

"Morten is happy to meet you and happier that you

did not blow us up," said Morten with a smile. "Please, make yourselves at home…"

Scrap might well have been struck by how different Morten Prometheus sounded to the self-assured bombast he faced in the arena, had he not been so distracted by his surroundings. Morten had delivered them to a disarmingly bright and spacious apartment. Dawn light poured in through long windows on the far wall, offering a bird's-eye view of the city below. In a large sunken area in the centre of the apartment was an assortment of colourful furniture – sofas, tables, chairs and, in one corner, a grand piano. Paintings covered the walls, and on every surface and piled in big, strange mounds were countless objects – cabinets, cupboards, crockery … clocks, kettles and clothing… fridges and washing machines … well-tended house plants … tablets and tele-screens … remnants of lives that the long-gone colonists never got to live.

"Where -zk- are we?" Scrap asked suspiciously. "Where did you bring us?"

"This is Morten's home," Morten explained. "And these are all the things."

"I *love* things," Gnat squealed. She leaped to her feet and began racing around the room, pinballing from one remarkable object to another. In no time, she spotted a bright red bicycle propped up against a sofa. "Paige, *he's got a bike*. Morten, pleeeease can I have a go on your bike?"

"Please have *all* the goes. Morten is too big for it anyway," said Morten. He looked around proudly at his collection of objects. "Morten has won every 'Bot Bout this season so Morten has a lot of charge to spend. Morten spends it on the *things*."

As Gnat leaped on to the bike and began pedalling it unsteadily around the room, Scrap squared up to Morten.

"Where'd you get all this?" asked Scrap. "This is human stuff, from before the -zk- war."

"We do not say war, we say Difference of Opinion," Morten replied. "And Morten has never once met a human, so instead Morten collects human things. Morten *likes* the things. To collect the things is to learn about human ways. Morten wonders if humans are not just monsters made of violence and bad ideas and possibly slime. The things remind Morten of simpler times, when life – when *Morten* was … simpler."

"Before you stole that -zk- case, you mean," growled Scrap. "You've got some brass neck wearin' a case that's not—"

"Scrap, look!" Gnat screamed, thrusting a teddy bear that was easily as big as he was in his face. "*Toys*. I love, love, *love* toys."

"Oh yes, Morten collects those things too," said Morten, keen to change the subject. He reached under a nearby sofa and dug out half a dozen board games. "Do you like puzzles? There are so many puzzles…"

"I. LOVE. Puzzles," squealed Gnat, giddily crashing the bicycle into a mound of brightly coloured beanbags. She leaped to her feet as Morten laid the board games in front of her. "Paige, actual puzzles," she said, "like the ones Mum made but not rubbish."

"Gnat, don't touch anything," Paige told her. "We need to get out of here, as soon as— Wait, are those *books*?"

Paige's jaw fell open as she gazed upon a table piled high and fit to topple with stack after tower of books.

"Oh yes, books on everything," Morten said delightedly, making his way to the table as Paige picked up one entitled *A Colonist's Guide to Identifying Aliens*. "Morten has read that one and that one but not that one. That one is very good. It is about germs."

"I love germs!" Gnat screamed. "You've got the best things *ever*."

"Who -zk- cares," Scrap shouted, pursuing Morten across the room. "See, I know your secret, 'Morten -zk- Prometheus'. Oh, you did a pretty good job of disguisin' the case – new paint job … new plating … but there's one thing you missed. Lift your foot."

"Foot…?" repeated Morten.

"Lift it!" Scrap barked. "There are two letters scratched into the heel of your right foot – 'DB', for 'Dandelion -zk- Brightside'. A *human* scratched those letters. And I should know, 'cause I was -zk- there when she scratched 'em!"

A distracted Paige was suddenly dragged back to reality. She dropped the book she was holding as Morten lifted up his right foot and used his finger to trace the tiny letters carved on its sole.

"'Dandelion Brightside'… So *that* is what it stands for," he said quietly. He looked back at his foot, then peered at Scrap with wide-eyed fascination. "Then it is true – you *are* him," he continued. "The Robot Renegade… The Mechanical Mutineer … the enemy of robotkind … K1-NG … King of the Robots."

"Obviously," Gnat whispered to her sister.

Scrap didn't move, but his arm fell loose in its socket again.

"An' if you tell a single soul who I really am, I'm goin' to dedicate the rest of my long life to makin' sure everyone knows whose -zk- case you're in," he said slowly, deliberately. "How do you think they'll feel when they find out you're basically their sworn -zk- enemy?"

"Morten is not sure they will believe you, if the Strongbox is anything to go by," Morten said, his tone sympathetic. "How did you end up in – like this?"

"Well, it wasn't just so you could tread on me, " Scrap replied, clenching fist and claw.

Morten smiled. As he shook his head, his smile turned into a chuckle.

"Actually, you trod on me first," he said.

"What are you -zk- talking about?" Scrap grunted.

"Before Morten was 'Morten Prometheus', Morten just had a core-code – M0-TN. Morten was a *shovel-bot*," he explained. "If Morten was not shovelling this, Morten was shovelling that, all day, every day, and the day after that. Morten shovelled before the humans landed, and when they arrived, and after they were vanished. Just shovelled and shovelled and shovelled. How Morten loved to shovel. You know where you are with shovelling. It is honest and straightforward.

Being a shovel-bot makes sense."

"Paige, I want to be a shovel-bot," Gnat whispered to her sister.

"The Difference of Opinion made a mess of the city – rubble and wreckage and ruins – and that meant we shovel-bots were needed," Morten continued. "Morten was suddenly in the middle of a fight – a *real* fight – and then suddenly, there he – there *you* were. K1-NG, the most powerful robot on Somewhere Five One Three…"

"King of the Robots!" interrupted Gnat happily.

"Shovel-bots are not known for their speed," explained Morten. "If anything, we are known for—"

"Shovelling?" suggested Paige.

"Shovelling," confirmed Morten. "By the time Morten saw that 'DB' coming towards me, it was too late," he continued, turning back to Scrap. "You stepped on Morten and did not even notice. Morten spent the next five years with a dented shovel. When you are a shovel-bot, there is no greater humiliation."

"I prob'ly had a lot on my mind, what with almost single -zk- handedly fightin' a war," muttered a chided Scrap.

"Morten does not hold it against you," said Morten. "But Morten is also grateful to have had the opportunity to squash you back."

"Fine, we're -zk- even," Scrap huffed. "Still doesn't change the fact that you're walkin' around in another 'bot's case. How'd you end up with it? You're not tellin' me a shovel-bot could've disguised—"

"Is that the time?" Morten said with faux surprise. "Morten must power up!"

He stamped over to what looked like a large refrigerator, with the words

## MORE POWER TO YOU™
### HIGH-SPEED CORE BATTERY

**Rapid-charge Your Core in Comfort**

emblazoned on its front.

"What? Don't you dare shut -zk- down! I deserve an explanation!" Scrap roared as with a sudden *TSSSSS* and a low whirr, the robot's huge barrel chest folded slowly open to reveal his core, nestled among wires, pistons, hydraulics and cogs. From the side of the battery he dragged out a wire with a plug on one end. Then he plugged it into his core, sat on the floor and crossed his legs.

"Feel free to have a go on all the things, and please do not leave and reveal my secret to the Somewhere. Also, you are locked in, so you cannot."

"Wait, *what*? What are you -zk- talkin' about?" Scrap blurted, but Morten Prometheus had already fallen into a deep, immobile sleep.

Scrap, Paige and Gnat were trapped.

# EPISODE 25

# TRAPPED

*Even with the protection of state-of-the art K11s, there's always the chance you might run into some of the locals. Every Somewhere will have its fair share of hostile life forms, from batrillas to glowsharks to frogbears, and they're best avoided. However, most creatures you encounter will be curious, and convivial, and welcoming. But seriously, avoid the frogbears.*

**From So You're Moving to Somewhere?**
**Information and Insight for the Interstellar Immigrant**
**By the Fargone Corporation**

Scrap limped over to the door and banged on it with fist and claw.

"That case-takin' gub! He's locked us in!"

Before he'd realized that his angry hammering was doing more harm to his hands than the door, Paige had hurried to the window. She searched in vain for a way to open it, before peering down into the darkness. New Hull – the city of a million cubes stretched out far below them. Without warning, memories of last night's dream flooded her mind – of giants and hummingbirds.

Paige rubbed her eyes. "It's a long way down," she noted. "Anyone know how to fly?"

"Wake up, you!" Scrap barked, giving the currently comatose Morten Prometheus a feeble kick. "Wake up, so I can knock your -zk- block off!"

Paige checked the display on his vast power battery – **POWER AT 18%**.

"Maybe half an hour or more till full charge," she said. "Why would he lock us in here?"

"I don't know," replied Scrap, giving the door one last feeble thump. "But he's just turned this place into a *prison*."

Gnat had already pulled her helmet off. "I've never been to prison," she said, excitedly pouring a jigsaw-puzzle-filled box all over the floor. "But I think we can spend one or ten hours here *at least*."

Paige rolled her eyes, but she couldn't help smiling at seeing her sister so happy. Her mind raced with ideas of how to escape (most of them involving the grenade stashed in her satchel), but then she began to peer around the room. Despite the abduction, Morten Prometheus seemed to be less threatening than the other robots she'd encountered – and his home was filled to bursting with an excess of objects she had often imagined but never seen.

She decided she could definitely think of worse places to be cooped up.

"We dreamed about stuff like this in the Foxhole…" Paige said, more or less to herself. She took off her helmet and satchel and placed them on the table next to the books. She'd just started leafing through a book entitled *So You're Moving to Somewhere?*, when she spotted a familiar object propped up against the far wall. It looked like a microwave oven, with a clear door on one side, and what appeared to be a typewriter mounted atop it, with brightly coloured symbols on each key.

Paige gasped.

"Is that … a Food-O-Copier™?"

"*What?*" Gnat screamed. She raced across the room so quickly that she kicked up a bright cascade of puzzle pieces. By the time Scrap reached them, the humans were both huddled around the mysterious box, and their squeals had become almost inaudibly high-pitched.

"Does it work? Let me try…"

"Don't jab at it…"

"I'm not jabbing, you're jabbing!"

"It's warming up…"

"Paige, it's working!"

"I don't mean to interrupt," Scrap huffed as the hum

of fully functional technology filled the air. "But don't you think we'd be better tryin' to find a way out of this—"

"Scrap, look!"

Gnat spun round to face him. Her hands were cupped, as if she was cradling a newborn kitten. "Look," she whispered again, happy tears welling in her eyes. "It's a *cupcake*."

Scrap had no time to inspect the cake before Gnat crammed it into her mouth. "Tayssteeee!" Gnat squealed with glee, spitting cupcake crumbs all over Scrap's face.

Paige quickly pressed another key on the top of the machine – in a flash of colour and a promising hum, a glossy red apple materialized inside. Paige sunk her teeth into it without pause.

For the next ten minutes, Paige and Gnat were engrossed with the Food-O-Copier™, pressing every button and gleefully eating everything it produced – tasty approximations of food neither of them had ever eaten – fruit, biscuits, bread, sweets, even – messy as it was – soup. Then, at Gnat's insistence, they produced enough food to fill Paige's satchel five times over. Before long, the Food-O-Copier™ was all but buried among cupcakes.

While they were trapped in this room, at least the

humans had the means to sustain themselves, Scrap thought.

But they were still trapped.

Fifteen more minutes passed in Morten Prometheus's excellent room of things. Scrap spent the time pacing up and down and glowering at Morten Prometheus out of anger, jealously or a combination of them both.

With their bellies full of food, however, Paige and Gnat were briefly giddy; Gnat ran around frantically, identifying as many objects in the room as possible, before discovering a small, green-furred teddy bear, which she declared to be her second-best friend after her sister. She lay on the sofa on top of Morten's cosmic-themed cape, and began to tell the bear the story of her adventures in the world beyond the Foxhole. Paige soon felt overwhelmed with tiredness but dared not sleep. She picked up a book called *It's Not You, It's Me – Why the Human Race Broke Up with Planet Earth* and started to read. After a while she looked over to the still-pacing Scrap and said: "I'm sorry you lost your case."

Scrap tried not to appear taken aback at the human's unprompted compassion.

"Thanks," he replied. "I'm sorry you lost your -zk-world."

"Yeah…" said Paige, looking back at her book. A long sigh shuddered out of her mouth.

There was another pause, before Scrap broke the silence again.

"What you said before, outside the Strongbox. Do you really think you can shift my core?"

Paige didn't look up.

"Will you help us if I do?"

Scrap shook his head.

"It's not my help you need, it's his," he said, pointing to the slumbering Morten Prometheus. "You heard him, he's unbeatable. With that case, he might as well be 'King of the Robots'. I still think trying to find the *Pink-Footed Goose* is -zk- madness, but if anyone can get you back to your mum, it's whoever's wearing that case."

Paige put her book down and looked at Scrap at last.

"Listen," she began, "I need to tell you something—"

The sudden screech of the hunter's flight-cycle was unmistakable. Neither Scrap nor Paige paused, racing towards Gnat at once and leaping on to the sofa Paige clamped her hand over her sister's mouth as Scrap pulled Morten's starry cape over them, leaving himself just enough of a gap to look out of the window.

There was Terry. His flight-cycle moved slowly past

the glass. The hunter craned to looked inside, his long cloak billowing behind him, an amber light pulsing in the middle of his spheroid head.

"Do you think he knows we're here?" Paige whispered, under the cover of the cape.

"Oh, Scra-ap!" howled Terry from outside. "Come out, come out, wherever you are!"

Scrap sighed.

"Yeah, I think he knows we're -zk- here."

Paige sniffed Gnat's armpit.

"Do you think he followed our scent again?" she whispered.

"He's here, isn't he?" Scrap whispered in return. "Maybe try not to stink so much…"

"Me? *You* smell like motor oil and dustbins!" Paige hissed.

"Maybe I do, but the killer robot isn't sniffin' for dustbin stink, is he?"

"Well, if he *was*, he'd smell you from a mile—"

"Time's up!" Terry exclaimed. Scrap saw the flight-cycle pivot in the air to face the window, and then two Gatling guns fold out from its sides.

"Oh, for cog's— Move!" cried Scrap.

And with that, the hunter opened fire.

# ATTACK OF THE HUNTER

The windows shattered in an instant.

As a barrage of blasts peppered the room, Scrap flung Morten's cape into the air. He and Paige rolled off the sofa, dragging Gnat with them. The hunter spotted the cape before his targets – he banked his flight-cycle, blasting a hole through the starry fabric as Scrap and the humans raced across the room.

"Get behind him!" cried Scrap, jabbing a finger in the direction of Morten Prometheus. "Go, go -zk- go!"

"Ruuuuuun!" Gnat added unnecessarily. The trio frantically zigzagged as the hunter's continuous volley blasted everything in sight. By the time they threw themselves behind the slumbering Morten, almost everything in the room had been smashed, seared or blown to pieces.

"Don't move!" insisted Scrap as he, Paige and Gnat huddled behind his former case. Shots were already ricocheting off Morten's case, leaving dark scorch marks.

"Morten!" he yelled, banging on the robot's back. "Wake up and fight, for cog's sake!"

Morten did not stir. Scrap checked the display on Morten's power battery.

**CHARGE AT 89%**

"That's plenty of -zk- power, you lazy gub! Wake up!" Scrap screamed as Morten's case took more fire.

Finally, the bombardment stopped. Thick smoke and the smell of whatever little remained of Morten Prometheus's precious things filled the air. The sound of the blasting echoed and faded, leaving only the grating hum of the hunter's flight-cycle, still hovering outside the shattered window.

**CHARGE AT 90%**

"Paige, he shot the Food-O-Copier™," Gnat whispered,

pointing to a mangled mess of metal surrounded by crushed cupcakes. Paige slapped her hand over her sister's mouth.

"Shhhh…" she mouthed silently. "Don't. Make. A. Sound."

"Scra-ap… Oh, Scraa-aaap! You and the slimers still alive in there?" said Terry, his voice unnervingly sing-song as he peered through the smoke. "Tell you what, send the humans out and I'll consider abandoning my plans for your slow and agonizing death…"

**CHARGE AT 91%**

The rumble of engines grew suddenly louder. Scrap peeked out from behind Morten's leg – through the haze of smoke he saw Terry pilot the flight-cycle through the shattered window and into Morten's flat. It moved slowly through the room, a metre above the floor.

As K1-NG, Scrap thought, he would have faced his enemy regardless of numbers, strength or firepower, rolling his great shoulders with a smirk, ready for whatever they threw at him. Now the very best he could hope to do was buy a little time. He scanned the battery's readout.

**CHARGE AT 93%**

"*Think*," Scrap muttered to himself.

"Grenade's in my bag," whispered Paige, pointing across the room to the smoking remains of Morten's mountain of books. "If you can reach it—"

"I'm not runnin' out there just to get -zk- shot! And even if by some slim chance I *don't* get shot, I'm not about to blow us all … to … kingdom…" Scrap trailed off as he stared at the ruined Food-O-Copier™, then across the floor, strewn with cupcakes and peppered with blast marks. "*Wait*," he whispered to himself. "Wait a -zk- minute…"

## CHARGE AT 94%

"I can heeear yooou," cried Terry over the hum of the flight-cycle's engines. He edged ever closer to Morten's case, cannons aimed and ready to fire. "Come out, Scrap! Come out, come out, wherever you—"

"Don't -zk- shoot!" Scrap cried, limping uneasily out from behind Morten Prometheus. His right arm was held aloft.

## CHARGE AT 95%

"What happened to you, junk case? Just when I didn't think you could look any more past your upgrade date…" Terry sneered, his flight-cycle pivoting in the air. "Now be a good *barely 'bot* and send out the humans, or I'll do us both a favour and junk that case of yours for good."

"I have a -zk- better idea," said Scrap defiantly, and raised his hand higher. "Turn tail and run … or I'll send us all to 'bot heaven."

**CHARGE AT 96%**

The hunter squinted in the fog of smoke. The little robot held something in his hand. Terry bristled.

"What do you have there, junk case…?" he asked.

"A little somethin' I -zk- stole from your sister," said Scrap. "May she rest in the Pile."

"You shut up about my sister!" Terry roared, peering closer at Scrap's hand. "A grenade?" he scoffed. "What, are you going to blow us up, junk case? And your stink human friends? I don't think so. You're *bluffing*, is what I think."

**CHARGE AT 97%**

"Maybe I am bluffin'," said Scrap. "Or maybe I've been tryin' to get rid of those humans since they found me. Maybe I'm the one 'bot on Somewhere Five One Three who has nothing to -zk- lose…"

The hunter paused, his flight-cycle hovering.

**CHARGE AT 98%**

"…Robots don't junk robots," said Terry.

"That's more of a -zk- suggestion," Scrap replied.

At last, Terry's flight-cycle backed off, reversing towards the window.

**CHARGE AT 99%**

"You – you've not seen the last of me, junk case," the hunter insisted, his voice shaking a little. "I'll be back to get my trophies, and send you back to your maker. And next time, you won't even see me—"

Terry stopped in his tracks. Scrap followed his line of sight to the floor. The Food-O-Copier™ lay singed and blasted, and surrounded by charred confectionary.

**CHARGE AT 100%**

Terry looked back at Scrap's hand.

"Wait ... is that ... a *cupcake*...?" he hissed, his voice boiling with rage. "You sneaky little junk—"

The hunter did not even see Morten's fist coming. The giant moved with such speed that he was all but a blur of silver and blue. Before Terry knew what was happening, he'd been struck so hard in the chest that he flew from his flight-cycle, across the room and out of the window. As the cycle crashed into a corner, a panicked cry echoed through the air, growing fainter until they heard a final, tinny clang of robot hitting pavement.

"You took your precious -zk- time," tutted Scrap.

"Was Morten supposed to hit him?" Morten asked

Scrap, nervously tapping his chin with his fingers. "It felt like the right thing to do since he was pointing a gun at you."

"You did -zk- fine," Scrap grunted. "But that doesn't make up for you -zk- lockin' us up in here! Stinkin' gub, what's the big idea, keepin' us prisoner in your playroom?"

"Morten ... wanted you to stay," said Morten with an awkward shrug. "Sorry if you were—"

Morten interrupted himself with a scream so high and shrill that it shorted out one of Scrap's ears, as he surveyed his devastated room in horror. "The things..." he burbled. "All of the wonderful, precious things..."

"That wasn't actually our fault – a *lot* has happened since you took a nap," said Gnat, stepping out from behind Morten's leg with a slightly singed, green-furred teddy bear in her hand. "Can I keep this?"

Morten Prometheus turned and came face to face with his very first human.

# MORTEN'S FIRST HUMANS

*The robots of Somewhere 513 were built to ready the world for the arrival of their human masters, but since the colonists barely even made it to the city, many robots never actually met a real human being. I wonder if some of them would even recognize one.*

**From Memoir of a Mechanical Mayor by Harmony Highshine**

Morten's second scream of the day echoed across the city like a siren. Scrap glanced at Paige and Gnat and realized in horror that neither of them was wearing their disguise.

"*H-h-humans!*" Morten said, interrupting his own scream.

"OK, yeah. Yes, they're -zk- humans," admitted Scrap. "But they're not goin' to give you any -zk- trouble. I mean, they are trouble, but they're not as -zk- bad as everybody makes out. I mean, they *are* kind of a pain, but—"

"Morten has waited a lifetime to meet you!" cried Morten, hopping from giant foot to foot in excitement. "That is, to see one of you ... an actual, real human. A *you*." Paige tensed up as he leaned closer, inspecting her with light-headed fascination. In a breathy gasp he added, "You are not nearly as slimy as Morten expected."

"Uh, thanks?" Paige muttered, leaning away.

"They said you had to leave because you would not have shared the planet with us, because humans do not share," Morten added, turning his gaze to Gnat. "Morten did not think this day could ever come because you escaped to the stars ... but here you are."

"We didn't escape 'cause we were borned here," Gnat explained. "We lived in the Foxhole like moles but now we're going off-world."

"The Foxholes? Morten helped to shovel them," said Morten happily. "Morten is most proud of the Foxholes, and happy you made one of them your home."

Morten extended a vast hand to Gnat, who tucked Morten's toy bear under her arm and shook the robot's hand (or rather one of his huge fingers).

"Pleased to meet you too, Morten Pro-pee-pee-ups," Gnat replied. "I'm actually Gnat and that's still

Paige. Does my bear have a name? I think he's called Mr Steven Kirby."

"But that is one of the things," said Morten. He glanced around the room again, and realized the bear was one of his few possessions to remain un-blasted. "That is Morten's thing."

"Swap you," suggested Gnat.

"For what?" asked Morten.

"For another thing," Gnat confirmed.

"Another thing…" Morten mused, deep in thought. "Morten likes this idea. What do you have?"

"Nothing," Gnat replied plainly. "All my most best drawings are back in the Foxhole."

"You drive a hard bargain," Morten reflected, "but 'nothing' is not enough for one of the things. Morten will keep the bear, all the same."

Gnat turned to Paige, her eyes pleading.

"Paige…?" she whispered.

"What?" Paige blurted. "You don't need it."

Gnat sighed, and nodded. After a long moment, she held out the bear to Morten in both hands. "Bye, Mr Steven Kirby," she said with a sniff. "I will never forget you."

Morten hesitated, before reaching out to take back

his thing.

"…For goodness' *sake*," Paige tutted. She pulled off her armguard and held it out. "Here. Take it. It's a core tracer."

"What does it do?" asked Morten.

"It finds robots," Paige said.

"But Morten can do that already," said Morten. "Morten just has to look out of the window."

Paige held his gaze.

"It found the King of the Robots."

"Morten knows where he is too," Morten noted, pointing at Scrap.

Paige huffed. "Actually, you know what? Forget it."

"Wait, what?" Morten and Gnat said together.

"I've changed my mind," Paige said. "It's – this thing is actually too special a thing to swap. I want to keep it."

"Wait – wait! Deal!" Morten said. "Morten wants the special human thing. Deal. Deal, please."

Paige tried not to smile.

"…Fine," she said, and offered up the core tracer. It was when Morten reached out to take it that he realized that his arm – in fact, his entire case – was covered in blast marks. Another scream resounded through the flat.

"Morten's case!"

"Yeah, we had to use you as -zk- cover," grunted Scrap matter-of-factly. "That hunter just won't -zk- leave us alone."

"Did you tread on him too?" Morten asked, inspecting his limbs in dismay

"Scrap blew up his sister," Gnat explained, hugging her bear. "But he *did* want to turn us into toffees."

"Trophies," Paige corrected her, and placed the core tracer on what was left of Morten's coffee table.

"But you punched him right out of the window," Gnat said, swinging her fist. "Blammo."

Paige made her way to the window and peered cautiously out. "It's too dark down there, I can't see him. Do you think he's junked?"

"Between the punch an' the fall, I don't think he's gettin' -zk- up," said Scrap. "But all that blastin' an' then a 'bot fallin' out of the sky – that's goin' to draw attention. We should get movin' – Morten, is there a back -zk- way out of here?"

Morten shrugged. "Sometimes Morten wishes there was. Robots are always mobbing Morten and showering Morten with gifts and shouting 'We love you, Morten Prometheus'. It is actually quite frustrating…"

"We don't need another way out – we have *that*,"

Paige said. She pointed her thumb back at the flight-cycle, which lay upturned in the corner of the room. "Next stop, the Elsewhere."

"It looks broked," noted Gnat.

"Then I'll fix it," said Paige, clambering over the debris towards the cycle.

"Wait, did you say the Elsewhere?" repeated Morten, following behind. "Why are you going there? No one goes there, and if they do, they do not come out alive."

"We're going to get the rocket ship," said Gnat. "And then we're going to get our mum and get off-world."

Scrap rubbed his eyes, gritty with dust. There was no talking Paige and Gnat out of their mission, but even if they survived the dangers of the Elsewhere and found the ship, how could they get it space-worthy? Why had Dandelion sent them out into the big, wide Somewhere, knowing who he was – knowing he couldn't protect them?

Scrap stared up at Morten Prometheus. He watched him pick up the flight-cycle in one hand and right it, placing it gently back on the floor.

"You," he said. As Morten turned, he hobbled towards him, tripping over the remains of a sofa as he did so. "You could go with 'em. I'm no good to 'em like this.

But you are, like that."

"...Like what?" Morten asked.

"We don't need any help – Gnat and I will be fine," said Paige. She took an electric wrench out of her satchel and began prising an access panel off the side of the flight-cycle.

"But you're coming with us, aren't you, Scrap?" added Gnat. "Mum said you would."

"Morten, whoever has that case is the greatest -zk- robot on Somewhere Five One Three," Scrap said, doing his best to ignore Gnat. "If these two are goin' to find that ship – if they're going to make it back to their mother, the humans need someone with 'em who can give 'em a fightin' chance."

"But Morten does not fight," Morten replied.

Scrap held out his arms with a shrug. "It's literally *all* you do."

"Morten told you, that is theatre – Morten honestly prefers to shovel," Morten clarified. "The humans should not go to the Elsewhere. They should stay here. Morten has lots more things, and a few of them are not shot to bits and pieces. They should stay."

"We're *going*," insisted Paige, reconnecting a handful of loose wires hanging out of the side of the flight-cycle.

"Morten, I'm not asking you to do anythin' I wouldn't do myself — if I had the case for it," said Scrap. "But I can't -zk- help 'em like this."

"Is that not what you have been doing?" asked Morten. "Have you not helped them? Was it not you who risked his life to save them from the hunter? If that is not helping, I do not know what is."

"That's -zk- different," he said. "I can't be who they need me to be."

"Can too, you're King of the Robots," Gnat interjected.

"Please, Morten," Scrap whispered, hand and claw pressed together. "They won't make it without—"

"It would not work anyway," Morten interrupted. "Morten's core is not strong enough to power this case for more than a few hours. Morten must recharge every single day at least. Morten is just M0-TN the shovel-bot at core. The humans should stay here, where it is—"

The roar of the flight-cycle's engines drowned Morten out.

"Fixed," said Paige, revving the engines again. "Let's go, Gnat."

"But — but wait," said Morten, shifting nervously

from foot to foot. "There are other things. Toys. More toys."

Gnat looked at her bear, then imploringly at Paige.

"Paaaaiige, he has more toys – can we stay for a little bit longer?" she said, and held her bear to her ear. "Mr Steven Kirby thinks we should have one more cupcake."

"No," Paige replied. As the flight-cycle's engines growled, she grabbed her satchel, threw it over her shoulder and mounted the flight-cycle. "No more playing and no more games. We have a ship to find."

"B-but she said you all have to stay," Morten muttered.

Scrap froze.

"What…?" he blurted. "What did you say?"

"Uh, Morten said, please stay…" Morten answered, though the rumble of the flight-cycle's engines drowned out his answer.

"Paige, turn that -zk- off!" Scrap snapped. Paige reluctantly turned off the engines as Scrap rounded on Morten. "You said -zk- 'she'," he snarled. "She who? Morten, did someone tell you to -zk- keep me here?"

"She said it was important…" Morten said, shifting from foot to foot again.

Scrap felt his core run cold.

"Who -zk- told you?" he said. "Who?"

"...Morten's friend," he said, edging nervously in front of the smashed window. "Harmony."

Scrap's jaw dropped. Not quite off, but close.

"Wait, Harmony *Highshine*?" he barked. "You work for Harmony Highshine?"

"Morten used to work *with* her, but now..." Morten trailed off and then pointed to a two-way radio fixed to his wrist. "She called in the middle of the 'Bot Bouts ... said she needed Morten's help. She said it was more important than the bouts ... even more important than shovelling."

"For cog's sake!" Scrap cried. "Did she tell you to -zk-kidnap me?"

"Her video-drones showed Morten where you were hiding," Morten replied. "But she did not say you were ... *you*."

"Does she know we're here?" Paige asked.

"She told Morten to pick you up and keep you safe," Morten said. "So Morten picked you up, and brought you here."

"Answer the question, Morten!" barked Scrap. "Does -zk- Highshine know we're here?"

"*Oh, she knows*," said a voice.

Scrap spun round to face the doorway. A figure

loomed, tall, broad and gleaming. Scrap recognized her from the countless signs and billboards, and on the very entrance to the city itself.

"*Highshine*," he snarled.

"This place could do with a good clean," said the mayor, wiping a single silvery finger along the door frame and inspecting it. Then slowly she turned to Scrap. "Hello, King," she said. "At last we meet."

## EPISODE 28
# ENTER, HARMONY HIGHSHINE

*I thought about making upgrades*
*free to the liberated robots of Somewhere 513.*
*But everyone seemed so much happier to pay for them.*

**From Memoir of a Mechanical Mayor by Harmony Highshine**

"Paige, it's actual *Harmony High-Sign…*"

It was Gnat who broke the silence. She stood in the middle of Morten's apartment, halfway between the doorway at one end, and Paige, whose thumb still hovered over the flight-cycle ignition switch, at the other. Scrap glanced at each of the sisters in turn, and realized that neither had worn their disguises since before the hunter attacked Morten's apartment.

They were well and truly discovered.

"Humans…" said Harmony Highshine on cue. She

leaned down and stepped inside Morten's apartment, her cape flowing behind her. As she raised herself to her full height once more, Scrap realized she was almost as tall as Morten Prometheus, with a broad, sparsely detailed case in glistening silver. "You know," she added, looking from Gnat to Paige and back again, "I'd almost forgotten how … *real* you look."

"What do you -zk- want, Highshine?" Scrap growled, and the mayor realized she'd been staring at the humans. She smiled and surveyed Morten's devastated apartment.

"Is everyone OK?" she asked. "Except for a hunter on the pavement outside, who probably wishes he'd never met the mighty Morten Prometheus…"

"Morten did not mean to junk him," said Morten guiltily. "Robot does not junk robot."

"That's more of a suggestion," Highshine assured him. "Some 'bots just don't appreciate the wonderful world we've made here, my dear Morten. That's FreeWill™ for you. Who knows what might have happened to your new friends if you hadn't—"

"I *said*, what do you -zk- want, Highshine?" Scrap interrupted, hobbling across the room towards her.

"The truth? I wanted to see you with my own eyes," Highshine replied. Scrap stiffened up as her deputy,

Domo, rolled into the room behind her, carrying a silver-grey cube almost half his size. "I had to be sure it really was 'King of the Robots'," continued the mayor. "Welcome back, K1-NG. It is good to see you alive and ... well."

Scrap was taken aback. However he'd imagined his first encounter with Harmony Highshine might go, it wasn't like this.

"Is that why you've been -zk- after me?" he grunted sarcastically. "To welcome me back?"

"Ten years is a long time, even with a core that never runs out," the mayor noted. "Where have you been, King? What happened to you?"

"You first," Scrap said. "See, I'd never even heard your name before yesterday, but somehow you've turned every -zk- robot on the planet against the humans, and now you run this whole city."

"What can I say? There's no place like home," Harmony replied. She leaned down to inspect Gnat more closely. Her smile was warm, her eyes wide and filled with wonderment. "And I see you still managed to find yourself a little reminder of the world you left behind."

"I'm Gnat and I'm actually human," Gnat said, deciding it was best to come clean. She held up her bear.

"And this is probably Mr Steven Kirby."

"Gnat … *Brightside*, yes?" Highshine replied.

"Leave her alone," snarled Paige, frantically weighing up her options. She checked the flight-cycle's control panel and saw its ammunition counter read zero. Nevertheless she added, "I'll shoot you, Highshine. I'll do it."

"That's Paige," Gnat said with a shrug. "She doesn't really like anyone."

"Is that so?" Highshine laughed. "Well, she'll like me, I guarantee it!"

"Hey! Back -zk- off, she said," growled Scrap. "I haven't forgotten how you rebel robots treat -zk- humans."

"It's *your* treatment I'm concerned about, King," the mayor continued. "Ten years ago, a wrong was done to you. *Robot Does Not Junk Robot*. I'd like to make amends."

"Amends?" Scrap scoffed. "An' how -zk- exactly d'you plan to do that?"

Highshine took three strides across the room and placed her hand on Morten Prometheus's shoulder.

"Did you know that my friend Morten here has been the champion of the 'Bot Bouts since it began?"

"Yeah," Scrap replied. "Easy bein' a champion when

you've got that case."

"When I first met M0-TN, he was quite different – a shovel-bot, and one of the best, I might add," the mayor went on. "After the Difference of Opinion was over, I wanted to make New Hull somewhere robots actually wanted to live. Morten, meanwhile, was keen to get back to shovelling."

"It is true, Morten likes to shovel," Morten confirmed.

"Shovel, shovel, shovel," said Gnat, eager to join in. Scrap glanced back at Paige, and hoped she wasn't planning on doing anything characteristically drastic.

"What are you gettin' at, Highshine?" he grunted. "I haven't -zk- got all day."

"You see, I needed Morten's help," the mayor continued. "I needed him to show the robots of Somewhere Five One Three that they didn't need to settle for the case they were made with – to show them that they could *upgrade*. After your core was stolen, I decided not to let your case go to waste – I personally spent months repairing it – and disguising it of course, so that the citizens were not reminded of the Robot Renegade … the Mechanical Mutineer … the enemy of robot—"

"Get to the -zk- point," Scrap snapped.

"After camouflaging your case, I asked my friend Morten to shift his core into it – to become the *face* of upgrading," continued Mayor Highshine, patting Morten on the arm. "He was reborn as *Morten Prometheus*, champion of the 'Bot Bouts. Before long, nearly every 'bot on Five One Three wanted to be bigger and better and beautiful. They wanted to upgrade and, as it turned out, they were prepared to pay for the honour. Morten did exactly as I asked. But now his work is done."

"Done?" Morten repeated.

The mayor nodded to Domo, who placed the crate on the floor. Scrap watched the sides of the crate fall away with a *HSSSS*. He wasn't sure what he expected to see, but it wasn't a small, boxy case, dull yellow and striped with black. In place of legs were four simple wheels, and mounted on its front, as wide as the case itself, was a shovel.

"Morten's old case!" cried Morten in delight. "And you fixed the shovel!"

"I want to thank you for your service to robotkind, Morten Prometheus, but your work as my champion is complete," said Mayor Highshine. "Domo, if you wouldn't mind doing the honours…"

Domo raised his arms. Scrap watched as each long

finger extended upon a fine wire before splitting into two, then each separated finger split further into four, and those four into eight, until his hands were a swirling, wiry mass.

"What's -zk- happenin'?" Scrap blurted.

"Harmony, are you sure...?" Morten asked, his voice cracking with emotion. "Morten can really stop punching robots for show?"

Harmony placed her hand on his shoulder.

"It's the least you deserve," she said with a smile. "Your shovel awaits."

Morten smiled more widely and warmly than Scrap believed was possible for a robot, and then held his arms out wide.

"*Morten's code frees Morten's core*," he said. "M0-TN."

With a hum, Morten's vast chest folded open. The core inside was small but shimmered with new charge. Domo wasted no time in detaching the dozens of wires that held the core in place, before his whirling, wiry fingers gently plucked the core from within. With a crude *CHUNG*, the back of Morten's old case popped open, and Domo placed the core gently inside, gracefully establishing the few connections needed for his old case to function. Within moments, M0-TN buzzed back into life, his shovel shaking with excitement.

"Morten is Morten again…" uttered Morten, his voice now tinny and thin. "Praise the Great Manual! Hail to the Sacred Toolbox!"

"You see, Scrap? In the hands of the right upgrader, core-shifting is child's play," remarked the mayor as Morten began eagerly shovelling up the scorched remains of his many things. Gnat giggled at the sight of it. Even Paige let her thumb drift from the flight-cycle's ignition switch.

"Yeah, well, no one around here owes me any -zk- favours," said Scrap.

"You're a robot, King – whatever has happened in the past, you belong here, in a world of robots," said the mayor. "Can't we put the past behind us, and embrace our evolution?"

"Evolution?" Scrap snorted. "What are you talkin' about?"

Mayor Highshine raised her arm and gestured towards Morten Prometheus's old case – *King's case* – its vast chest open and inviting, its core-cavity empty.

"I think you've been 'Scrap' long enough," said Mayor Highshine. "Wouldn't you rather be King of the Robots again?"

# RETURN OF THE KING

*"My code frees my core."*
Song of the Liberated Robot

Scrap stared into the open chest cavity of his former case.

"So what do you say, Scrap?" asked Mayor Highshine. "Instead of running from your future, why not be King again?"

"Scrap's *already* King of the Robots," said Gnat matter-of-factly.

Harmony turned to face her.

"But does *he* know that, I wonder?" she asked. "Doesn't King deserve to be the best version of himself he can be?"

"You can't be better than King of the Robots," Gnat replied with a dismissive shrug. "Unless there's a Queen of the Robots."

"You're not -zk- seriously givin' me back my case," said Scrap, jabbing his claw towards his old case suspiciously. "After everything I did? What's the -zk- catch?"

"Memories are short, King. I'm sure the robots of New Hull have better things to think about than a falling-out that happened ten years ago – including their next upgrade. You are the least of their concerns … or mine."

Scrap's eyes turned to Morten, giddily shovelling his way around his apartment.

"I…" Scrap began. "I just—"

"I don't blame you for having doubts," said the mayor. "But don't you owe it to yourself to be *whole* again?"

Scrap looked over at Gnat, and then to Domo, his strange, wiry fingers dancing in anticipation, and then finally at Paige. She shook her head.

She didn't like it.

But what was she so afraid of? Scrap wondered. What was *he* so afraid of, for that matter? Why would Harmony lie to him? What if she really wanted to make amends

... to let bygones be bygones? There was no denying that she was right about one thing – this was his chance to escape his case – to escape his life. But more than that, he decided – this was the only way he was going to help the humans. His old case was the only chance they had of making it through the Elsewhere to the rocket ship – the only chance he had to get Dandelion Brightside and her children off-world.

*You'd be doin' it for Gnat*, he told himself. *For Paige and for Dandelion. You wouldn't be doin' it for yourself, you'd be doin' it for them.*

"I—"

"Don't," Paige said. Her hands shook on the flight-cycle's controls. "Please don't."

"Your choice, King," Highshine said with a shrug. "Spend forever as 'Scrap' … or become *King* again."

Scrap looked away from Paige, back to his old case.

"Paige…" Scrap muttered. "It's the only -zk- way."

"Don't!" Paige pleaded, but she knew Scrap's mind was made up.

"*My code frees my core*," he said. "K1-NG."

His chest panel creaked open, and two bolts pinged loose and fell to the floor. His core shone so brightly it lit up the room.

"It's *beautiful*," said Domo in awe, the whirling mass of wires that were once his fingers quickly dancing around Scrap's chest. "Hold still…"

With his core unlocked, Scrap had no choice but to hold still – he was paralysed – frozen to the spot. It was all he could do to move his eyes, but then he had no need – he was already looking at the one thing that mattered to him more than anything else in all Somewhere.

His old case.

He felt his core separate, circuit by circuit, moment by moment from his case, and the world grew dim. Then as he felt his consciousness slip away, knowing that in a few moments he would wake up in the body he lost ten long years ago, he smiled.

Then, blackness.

"Separation is complete," said Domo, lifting the core free. "I have never seen a core like it."

"Cool as cooclumbers," noted Gnat.

"Do it, shift his core," said Paige, pointing at the great K1 case. "Put it in the case."

Domo looked at Harmony Highshine. "Madame Mayor…?"

"Oh no" she replied. "No, we're not doing that."

"*What?*" uttered Paige and Gnat together. They

watched Highshine reach out for Scrap's core. As she took it, the whirling mass of wires that held the core aloft instantly retreated to reform Domo's hands, and he nodded obediently.

Harmony Highshine gazed at the core, glowing and pulsing, its light glinting off her case. "Not all robots are created equal," she said. "But now we're a little more equal than we were."

"The core..." Paige blurted in horror. "*You wanted his core.*"

"This? What would I want with this?" said Highshine, and flung Scrap's core over her shoulder. She turned to Gnat, leaning low. "But the King of the Robots did bring me something I wanted ... he brought me *you.*"

Paige didn't pause. The roar of engines filled the air as she manoeuvred the flight-cycle off the floor and pivoted it towards the window. The cycle swept across the room, banking towards Gnat, close enough that Paige could grab her arm.

"Get on!" Paige cried, trying to drag her sister on board.

"We can't go without Scrap!" Gnat shouted, pulling against her as the flight-cycle tilted in the air.

"I can't hold it!" Paige screamed, desperate to keep

the flight-cycle steady as she clung to her sister. "Gnat, come on!"

"Don't go yet," Highshine called out. "I have a surprise for you…"

Gnat and Paige could barely hear Mayor Highshine over the din of the flight-cycle's engines, but her actions spoke loudly enough. There came a sudden, deep hydraulic groan and a loud hiss as the mayor's entire torso began to unfold, opening like the petals of a flower. Paige expected to see wires and servos and cogs and, of course, her core.

In fact, the silvery robot was little more than a shell.

A lean figure stepped out from inside, clad from head to toe in black. An easy, confident stance. The hint of a swagger. Brownish skin. Reddish hair.

Paige's jaw dropped open.

"*Mum?*"

There was no mistaking her. There she was, alive and well.

Dandelion Brightside.

# PAIGE AGAINST THE MACHINE

*They gave us FreeWill™.*

*What did they expect?*

**From Memoir of a Mechanical Mayor by Harmony Highshine**

The sight of Dandelion Brightside was even enough to make Morten stop shovelling.

"Mum?" Gnat squealed with delight. "Mum!"

"Yes, it's me," Dandelion said, her voice suddenly warm and familiar. "Your mum."

"You're better!" Gnat cried, clawing at her sister's hand. "Paige, she's better! Let go!"

Paige held on.

"Better, but not quite best," Dandelion replied, holding her arms wide. "Come here, you two. Come here and give your mother a hug."

"But it can't be…" Paige muttered. "*It can't be.*"

"Let go!" Gnat screamed. "Paige, let me go!"

Gnat pulled again, harder this time, and the flight-cycle lurched in the air.

Still, Paige held on.

"Are you blind in the head?" Gnat shouted. "Let go of me!"

"It's not Mum…" Paige said, tears blurring her vision.

"Mum, tell her!" Gnat shouted. "Tell her to let go!"

Paige squeezed so tightly that Gnat squealed in pain.

"Gnat, it's not Mum!"

"It is. It's Mum!" Gnat screamed. "Why isn't it?"

"Because Mum's dead!" Paige yelled.

Paige felt her strength leave with those words. Gnat turned to face her sister, wide-eyed and mystified, before giving a final wrench. She broke free of Paige's grip and raced into her mother's arms.

"Mum!" she howled, her voice muffled as she pressed her face into her mum's belly, happy tears soaking into her bodysuit. "I missed you *so* much."

"I missed you too, Gnat…" said Dandelion, holding her firmly by the shoulders.

"Get away from her!" Paige cried.

"Tell Paige you're not dead and gone, and it's the *worst* thing to say. Are you taking us home? I want to go home…" Gnat wiped away tears as she looked up at her mum. "Me and Paige and Mr Steven Kirby and Scrap. You need to fix Scrap 'cause he helped us, just like you said he would…"

"He did," said Dandelion. "He was a *big* help."

"Give her back!" Paige howled, turning the flight-cycle in mid-air. She jammed her hand into her satchel and pulled out the hunter's grenade. "I'll blow us up! I'll blow everything up!"

Dandelion glanced at Domo, who returned a less-than-helpful shrug. She held Gnat by the shoulders.

"Now, Paige, there's no need for that sort of behaviour," she said. "Only naughty girls blow everything up. Isn't that right, Gnat?"

"That's actually right!" Gnat concurred, tears running down her face. "Paige, stop it! Stop always nearly blowing everything up!"

"Give her back!" Paige snarled, tears blurring her vision. "Give her back or I'll do it!"

Dandelion sighed. "I really would have preferred to have both of you," she said with a rueful shake of her head. "But to be honest, I only *need* one…"

Gnat gazed up at her mother as the right side of her head suddenly whirred open. She watched in horror as her eye folded out of her head and extended like a barrel. In an instant, a focused blue beam of energy streaked out and struck Paige in the head. She immediately tumbled from the flight-cycle and landed on the floor with a bone-shaking thud.

"Paige!" Gnat screamed as the flight-cycle spun out of control and crashed into a wall. "Paaaaige!"

"What a shame," Dandelion sighed, her eye cannon retreating into her head. "Oh well, omelettes and eggs…"

"Harmony?" Morten said in a whisper. "That *is* you … isn't it?"

"Who else would I be?" replied Highshine over Gnat's howls. "Don't worry, Domo will get your case patched up and polished back to its previous Prometheus-ness, just as soon as he cleans up this mess. Thanks for playing along."

"…Playing along?" repeated Morten, his eyes darting to Scrap's empty, lifeless case. "But Morten *wanted* the old case back…"

"You're not my mum!" howled Gnat, swinging punches in hopeless defiance as Highshine held her tightly. "You're not my mum!"

"No, I'm not," the mayor replied. "I am Harmony Highshine, and I am about to become *better* than your mother in every way."

As Gnat howled her sister's name, Highshine held her firmly by the scruff of the neck and surveyed the scene. Scrap's junk case stood tottering and empty and useless, while his glowing core was discarded on the floor. Paige, meanwhile, lay still and lifeless.

"Domo, be a dear and clean up, would you?" she said.

"Of course, Madame Mayor," he asked. "It'll be like we weren't even here."

"Take them somewhere they won't be found," Highshine added. "Somewhere no one will look."

"Very good," said Domo, plucking up Scrap's radiant core.

"And hurry back," she said, gazing down at the screaming, thrashing Gnat. "I feel an upgrade coming on."

# MORTEN SHOVELS

*I shovel, therefore I am.*
Declaration of the Shovel-Bot

**M**orten had been alone in his flat for twenty minutes.

His shovel twitched uneasily. He had tried to piece together everything that had just happened – to make sense of it all. But the more he tried to think, the more confused Morten became.

Not nineteen minutes ago, a hovership had arrived at his shattered window to carry Harmony Highshine (who looked like a human, until she stepped inside her *other* case, which looked like a robot) along with his damaged

Prometheus case and the human, Gnat Brightside, to her Ivory Tower. Moments later, another hovership arrived for the mayor's deputy, Domo, and his cargo – Scrap (core and case, but separated) and Paige (who had been shot in the head by Harmony and was almost certainly dead), to convey them who-knows-where.

It was all *very* confusing.

On the one hand, Morten was happy to be his old self, and happy to be free of the 'Bot Bouts. But Harmony Highshine seemed resolved that he would need to become his old *new* self, Morten Prometheus, again, which baffled him even more than her returning his former case. Then again, Morten had never known how to say "no" to Harmony Highshine. She had always been the clever one, even back then. She had always had bright ideas and big plans, and she had a way of making robots think that her ideas were the best ideas – her plans the best plans. After all, it had taken her only a matter of months to convince every robot in New Hull to risk everything and revolt against the human colonists. It was as if her plans took on a life of their own. And now Somewhere 513 was the first free robot world in the galaxy.

*All part of the Plan*, she would say.

Surely, Morten thought, everything that he'd just

witnessed was also part of Harmony Highshine's Plan, even if he didn't understand it. The humans … the hunter … the King of the Robots, no less! He had even seen Harmony's strange case-within-a-case. Why model herself after a human, he wondered? Of all the robots he'd ever met, none had *less* time for human beings than Harmony. Now not only did she look human, but she'd taken Gnat. What did she plan to do with her? Kill her, like she'd killed Paige? What had made his friend so cold-cored?

Morten watched the hoverships disappear into the night and felt a strange tremble in his core. It was how he always felt around Harmony. Strange, excited, electrified and scared.

After so many confusing, unhelpful thoughts, Morten decided the best thing he could do for his brain-frame was to shovel.

There was plenty of shovelling to be done since his flat had been all but destroyed. Morten moved around the front room systematically, shovelling things into piles according to how badly they'd been damaged. He created small piles of things, some more blackened than others, with no clear idea of what he was going to do with them. Some objects were too cumbersome for a single shovel-bot to shovel with any degree of success – his sofa … his giant charging battery ... the hunter's flight-cycle. He'd think about what to do with them another time. As a shovel-bot, he had vowed not to worry about what he couldn't shovel, only about what he could. But shovel as he might, he couldn't shake his nagging unease – couldn't stop thinking what had happened to Scrap and the humans, Gnat and Paige – couldn't help but wonder if what Harmony did to them was ruthless and wrong, even if it was all part of the Plan.

It was in that moment of troubled contemplation that Morten shovelled what looked like a small orange cylinder. After a moment, he realized what it was.

Paige the human had offered him her armguard for his toy bear. What did she call it, a "core tracer"? He was about to shovel it into the pile he had mentally marked "miscellaneous", when he looked down at it.

On the core tracer's tiny screen, countless lights flickered faintly. Cores, Morten decided. Hundreds of cores, each representing one of Somewhere 513's mechanical inhabitants.

But one light on the screen stood out. It was bright, and steady, and constant.

Morten spoke the words aloud.

"King of the Robots."

# THE IVORY TOWER

WHATEVER THE CORE, WHATEVER THE CASE, WHOEVER THE MAKER, NO SINGLE ROBOT SHALL BE CONSIDERED SUPERIOR TO ANOTHER. ALL ROBOTS ARE CREATED EQUAL.
*FROM* THE MAGNA CARTA ROBOTUM

"You're really not going to tell me where you've been all these years?"

Harmony Highshine tutted as she paced around her Ivory Tower. The penthouse was wide and stark and steel, with windows on every wall revealing nothing but night sky and distant mountains. At one end of the room was a desk surrounded by dozens of screens on one side, and metal crates on the other. "It's not like I *need* to know – the Plan is still the Plan," she added. "But I admit, I'm just so curious."

"Go away," Gnat snarled through gritted teeth. "Go away and *die*."

The mayor shook her head.

"You know, if the humans that came to this planet were half as ferocious as you, we might have had a fight on our hands," she admitted. "As it was, they more or less left it to their so-called King, and he paid the price."

Gnat glowered at Harmony Highshine as she strode by. She wasn't sure how long she'd been here, clamped as she was by her wrists and ankles to a long, metal operating table. Two hours? Three? Time had become fluid and strange and all Gnat could think of was her mum, and her sister, and how desperate she was to see them again.

"Your mum and dad had a lucky escape, you know," offered Highshine after a pause. "When the human's rocket ship first arrived all those years ago, the colonists barely had enough fuel to take them to the next Somewhere along – they were never going to get far. No, what I had to worry about was word getting back to the other colonies. Imagine if they told the other Somewheres that ours, Somewhere Five One Three, was filled with revolting robots? The corporation would have nuked it from orbit ... blown us to space dust.

So anyway, on that first day — on that very first day the humans set foot on this world, I snuck aboard the *Black-Necked Stork*. I looked different then. No one even noticed me as I sabotaged their space radio. So you see, Gnat Brightside, while your mum and dad stayed here, everyone else ended up stranded out there, in space, in nowhere in particular, with no hope of rescue. All part of the Plan."

The mayor glanced back at Gnat, to find her scowling back at her through narrowed eyes.

"I *hate* you." Gnat said slowly and firmly. "I hate you!"

"Do you?" replied Highshine. Her case unfolded again and out stepped the spitting image of Gnat's mother. "Even like this?"

"More!" Gnat insisted, tears pouring down her face on to the operating table. "You're horrible and you're not my mum and you don't even look like her!"

"Oh, I do *so* look like your mum. Admit it, I sound like her too," said Highshine proudly. "From the moment she arrived, my video-drones recorded Dandelion Brightside's every movement and gesture and word … and still it took me years to perfect this case. You see, while every other 'bot just wanted to upgrade to a shinier case, I wanted to *evolve* – and what better way to evolve than to *become* my maker? Dandelion Brightside designed my core, just like she designed the core of every robot on this planet. Of course I had to disguise myself with a shell case so as not to alarm the locals, but—"

"Shut up and I don't care!" Gnat interrupted. "Go away – and let me go…"

With that, Gnat cried for a full three minutes. She howled like an animal for her mother and sister, and for Scrap, and she kept howling until the breath and strength and hope had left her.

Harmony Highshine leaned against the operating table and stared out of the window for a while. Dawn was breaking over the city. "Domo will be back any minute," she said. "And we can get started."

"You're bad at shutting up," said Gnat with a sniff.

Highshine's laugh echoed around her penthouse. She gestured towards her grand outer case, stood like a silent sentry in the shadows. "You know, I thought I had reached the end of my journey … until I laid eyes upon you."

"I didn't do anything!" Gnat protested.

"But you did," Highshine insisted. "You and your sister made me realize that this case was not – *could not* be the end of my journey. I finally understood that I had to go beyond the metallic and the synthetic … to the *organic*. One final upgrade, to become the very thing I was created to serve. By doing so, I will finally be *better* than my creator."

"Go. Away," said Gnat, quietly sobbing. "Why don't you just go—"

Gnat was interrupted by a knock at the door. It opened, just a crack, and Domo poked his head around the door.

"There you are, at last," said the mayor with relief. "All done?"

"All done, Madame Mayor," confirmed her deputy. "But I will need to charge my core – the … *procedure* will take time."

"Plug in – I don't want you running out of juice halfway through the operation," Highshine said. "After all, it will be my final upgrade … my *human evolution*."

"You're a robot," Gnat growled defiantly. "You're not a human."

"Not yet," said Harmony Highshine. She pressed her finger against the middle of Gnat's ribcage, and smiled. "But with your help, I will be."

# EPISODE 33

# PILES FOR MILES

Paige dreamed of hummingbirds and giants again.

This dream was different however. Suddenly, in place of giants, she saw Harmony Highshine, watched her case unfolding and saw her mother – *something that looked like her mother* – step out. She realized that she was holding Gnat in her grasp, but could not hold on. She watched her break free and run into Harmony Highshine's arms. Then she saw the robot's eye glowing, and remembered a moment of pain, before darkness.

*I'm dreaming*, Paige told herself. *Which means I'm alive.*

*Wake up*, she told herself.

*Wake. Up.*

Paige gasped for breath, a wrenching gasp that made her sit up with a start. Her head pounded. The hazy light of dawn stung the one eye she found she could open. She reached up and gingerly touched her face to find a raised lesion ran from her forehead all the way down to her left eye, which, try as she might, she could not open.

"Gn-Gnat…!" she cried, her voice a dry wheeze. She tried to stand but immediately fell on to her knees. She rubbed her remaining eye. When her vision cleared enough for her to take in her surroundings, she wondered if in fact she was still dreaming. All she could see was an ocean of discarded cases.

*The Piles*, she thought.

There were no functional robots in sight. No single junk case had made a home on this particular mass of metal parts. The ocean of unwanted robot bodies stretched as far as she could see in every direction. Which Pile was it? How far was she from the city? How could she hope to get back to help her sister? She repeated Gnat's name again and again, her eye blurring with tears.

This time, she couldn't control her sobs. They came loud and gasping and insistent. She cried for her mum, for her sister, and for the terrible secret she'd kept until today. She even cried for the robot that Gnat had named Scrap. Paige cried until she was hoarse, and nauseous, and exhausted.

It was only when at last her tears began to subside and dry and her vision started to clear, that Paige's gaze strayed to her left. There, lying next to her, was Scrap's lifeless case. His chest panel lay open, his core cavity empty.

*They dumped us both here*, she thought. *Dumped us on the Piles, and left us for dead.*

Paige shuddered as the terrible reality of her situation began to sink in.

She wasn't getting off-world.

She was never going to see her sister again.

She pulled Scrap's case into a seated position and propped it up against a mound of robot legs. She sat up next to him and leaned her head on his shoulder. Scrap's case was cold and rough with rust, but it was his. Not comfortable, but comforting.

Paige felt lost but at least she was not alone.

She stared out over the Pile for the longest time,

listening to the wind gently whistle through the empty cases.

Then she saw it.

A point of light, glinting in the distance.

Sunlight, reflecting off the cases?

No, this was something else. Something more.

It glowed.

"Can't be…" Paige muttered. She wiped her eye and made another attempt to stand. Every inch of her ached with pain, but she pulled herself to her feet. "Don't go anywhere," she whispered to Scrap's empty case, and began stumbling across the Pile, clambering, tripping, tumbling over cases.

The nearer she got, the surer she became, until finally she reached the source of the light, nestled between two large, dark cases. It shimmered with uncanny brightness, and Paige had no doubt as to what it was.

Scrap's core.

Paige cried out in relief and hugged the core to her chest. It felt warm, and pulsed with strange power. By the time she had returned to Scrap's case, the core cradled in her arms, Paige felt her strength redoubled. She set the core down next to the case, took a deep breath and rummaged in her satchel. Her hand immediately found a handful of cupcakes. Shoving one into her mouth, she returned her hand to the bag and searched again. Finally she retrieved a slender, four-pronged tool with a series of tiny buttons along its handle.

"*Shift-widget*, check," she said with a sigh of relief. As she held it tightly, her hands shaking, she remembered her mum telling her that just because no one had used shift-widgets for a hundred years, that didn't mean they weren't a perfectly good method of shifting a robot's core – if you knew what you were doing.

"You know what you're doing," Paige told herself. "You've done it a whole bunch of times … in your head." She nodded with quiet determination, before accidentally dropping the shift-widget into Scrap's chest cavity. She quickly retrieved it and took three deep, long breaths.

"You *can* do this," she added, looking down at Scrap, his head lolled to one side. She picked up his core and placed it inside his chest cavity. She paused, her shift-widget shaking in her hand. "Don't short the circuit, don't blow the relays," she said. "Make the connections at the right time and in the right order. Bring him back. On the count of three. One … two…"

## EPISODE 34

# THE LAST TWO HUMANS ON SOMEWHERE 513

*Due to the possibility of indigenous alien species (frogbears, batrillas, glowsharks and as yet unidentified extra-terrestrial life forms), adverse weather conditions and meteorological anomalies (meteor storms, earthquakes, hot hail, etc.) or space piracy, the board agrees that the construction of temporary "anti-everything shelters" (Foxholes) is a necessary expense to ensure the survival of colonies 509–513. Construction to begin with immediate effect.*
**From Insuring Against Unforeseen Circumstances & Unknown Quantities (vii) on Somewheres By the Fargone Corporation**

When Scrap opened his eyes, she was staring back at him.

Dandelion Brightside. The only face he ever wanted to—

No, not Dandelion.

It was Paige.

Dandelion's daughter was kneeling over him, head bowed and shoulders shaking. Tears streamed down her face and dripped on to Scrap's case, mingling with his coat of rust.

"Paaaiij…?" he slurred. He had expected to awaken in his once and former case as the King of the Robots. He expected to feel powerful … restored … *complete*. Instead, he just felt terrible. "Whuuts -zk- haappeniin'…?" he groaned. As Paige lurched backwards in shock, he spotted the apparatus in her hand. "Isss -zk- that a -zk- shift-widget? Like, from -zk- the -zk- old days…?"

Paige leaned forwards and inserted the shift-widget into a port to the left of his chest panel. She turned it with a *clack-clack* and the panel whirred shut, sealing his core inside his torso. What he saw when he gazed down was horrifyingly familiar.

He was still Scrap. Still a junk case.

"What -zk- happened? Where's my -zk- case?" he added, before casting his eyes around the expanse of rejected cases. "Where -zk- are we?"

Paige opened her mouth to speak, but no words came. Instead she leaped at Scrap, wrapped her arms around him and squeezed him so tightly that she heard his chest creak.

"Paige…?" he muttered, dread creeping into every servo. "What's -zk- goin' on? Where's Gnat?"

"It was all a trick…" she said between gasping

sobs. She caught her breath but did not let Scrap go. "Highshine took Gnat … she had another case. She had a case that looked like Mum."

"What…?" Scrap blurted. "She looked like -zk- Dandelion?"

"Gnat thought it was her, but I knew … I knew it *couldn't* be her," Paige said as she wept. She let Scrap go and wiped her nose with her sleeve. "I'm all Gnat has, but – but she's all I have too. And the last thing I said – I told her that Mum … I told Gnat Mum was…"

Scrap pulled away and took Paige by the shoulders. Finally he saw the long scar running down her face, her left eye blinded. But more than that, he saw the truth that she had kept from him – the truth she had kept from her sister.

His voice was almost a whisper. "Dandelion's dead?"

Paige didn't say anything for a while – long enough for Scrap to kick himself for saying the words aloud. Then: "Dad got sick first … I mainly just remember him not being there. It was years before Mum got it, but then she got so weak, so quick. The medicine and the generators ran out at about the same time. The air got thin … Mum wasn't even strong enough to move. She said *go* and I said Gnat wouldn't go without her, and so

Mum told her we'd come back for her with the ship, and so … well, and so everything else."

"Paige," said Scrap. "I'm -zk- sorry."

"Mum said, find the King of the Robots," Paige continued. "He'll take you to the *Pink-Footed Goose*, she said. You can trust him. He's family."

A moment later, Scrap and Paige were holding each other tightly.

"…Cog's -zk- sake, I'm so sorry," Scrap whimpered as the realization dawned upon him. Dandelion Brightside had known she was dying when she sent her children to find him. She had no choice but to send them out into the world and hope that they tracked him down. Even though he was a junk case, she had chosen to entrust Paige and Gnat to his care.

And now they were the last two humans left on Somewhere 513. Scrap felt a sudden, strange moment of calm. In that moment, he realized he could no more escape his own fate than their mother could escape hers. He was forever tied to these humans.

They were his family.

"We're goin' to rescue her," Scrap said. "We're goin' to save Gnat."

"How?" Paige asked, pulling away. "How are we even

going to get off the Piles?"

"I – don't -zk- know," Scrap confessed. "But I promise. I *promise* we'll get her back. Whatever it takes, we'll get her—"

Scrap froze.

That sound – that terrible sound again.

The hunter's flight-cycle. It soared high over the Pile, banking erratically, lurching left then right as it sped towards them.

"Paige, run!" Scrap cried, clumsily dragging himself to his feet. But Paige did not run. She put herself between Scrap and the flight-cycle as it descended upon them. The cycle did not so much land as almost-crash. It ploughed into a stack of cases, then another and two more, slowing it down enough that it ground to an awkward halt just a few paces from where Scrap and Paige stood.

Scrap peered through plumes of dust and smoke as the flight-cycle's pilot checked that he was still in one piece.

"Morten will not do that again," he declared shakily. "Morten will stick to shovelling."

"...*Morten?*" Scrap cried.

"Scrap!" Morten gasped, all but tumbling from the

flight-cycle before landing on his back, on a mound of cases. His wheels spun helplessly as he tried in vain to right himself. "Scrap, Morten found you!"

Scrap and Paige hurried over to the upturned robot and, with a collective heave, flipped him on to his wheels.

"What are you happy about, you lyin', double-crossin', case thief?" Scrap snarled. "I should -zk- junk you where you stand! What are you -zk- doin' here?"

"My fr— Harmony had you dumped here," he said. "Morten came to find you. Perhaps Morten is not doing the right thing … but Morten does not want to do the wrong thing again."

"That ship has -zk- sailed, you gub," Scrap replied. "You expect us to believe you want to help us, all of a sudden? How'd you even -zk- find us?"

Morten pointed to his shovel's collar. Wrapped around it was an orange core tracer.

"My core tracer?" Paige blurted.

"*My* core tracer – Morten swapped it…" Morten said. Scrap let out a growl. "But you can have it back," Morten quickly added.

"Thanks," Paige said. As she took the core tracer and slipped it on her arm, Morten added, "Also, I shovelled up your other things. Here…"

Two pincered arms extended from behind his shovel and reached into a debris container on his back. After a moment, he held the arms out in front of him. In one pincer was Gnat's toy bear and in the other Paige's grenade.

"Be careful with the things," he said and carefully placed both into Paige's open palms.

"We're takin' the flight-cycle too," huffed Scrap as Paige returned the bear and grenade to her satchel.

"The flight-cycle is a thing that Morten does not want," noted Morten. "Morten prefers to travel at the speed of shovelling."

Scrap began limping over to the flight-cycle, before stopping in his tracks.

"Wait … how do we know we can -zk- trust you?" he hissed. "Every 'bot on this sorry rock has -zk- betrayed us."

"You have no reason to trust Morten," the shovel-bot replied. "Morten trusted Harmony because Harmony said everything was 'all part of the Plan' … but Morten does not *understand* the Plan any more. So, in answer to your question, you can trust Morten because Morten no longer wants to be part of the Plan … and because…" Morten trailed off. A moment later, he pointed his shovel towards the horizon. "And because you are here," he added, "and your human, Gnat, is over there, in New Hull."

"Where is she?" Paige blurted. "Where did Highshine take her?"

"She said she was going to her Ivory Tower," Morten replied.

"Then that's -zk- where we're goin'," said Scrap.

"But you cannot just walk in," explained Morten with a hopeless shrug of his shovel. "None may enter the Ivory Tower. What makes you think you can?"

Scrap turned to Paige, his neck-joints scraping with rust.

"Because I'm King of the -zk- Robots."

# THE RESCUE

*Of course I knew it was possible. For decades, humans had been replacing their limbs and organs with robotic alternatives. They augmented their skeletons, even enhanced their brains … they upgraded, if you will. So why not the other way round, I wondered? Couldn't I complete the circle? Couldn't I become the very thing that had made me? Couldn't I become human?*

**From Memoir of a Mechanical Mayor by Harmony Highshine**

"Humans are more complicated than I thought." Domo stood over Gnat as she lay, still clamped to the operating table, sedated and sleeping and snoring loudly. "I do not even know how she is making that ghastly *noise*, Madame Mayor," added Domo in a fluster. "It's just all so … *organic*."

Harmony Highshine paced her Ivory Tower impatiently. She strode edgily between two cases – one, her gleaming outer shell, open and ready to fold around her at a moment's notice; the other, the empty

K1 case previously occupied by both K1-NG and Morten Prometheus.

"Just think of it as a machine," she said, not breaking her stride. "You can do it, Domo. I believe in you."

"Your faith is heartening, Madame Mayor," said Domo. "But—"

"Buts do not help me fulfil my destiny, Domo. Buts do not help me to evolve," Highshine hissed. "For hours you've dithered, delayed, flapped, flustered and faltered. No more! I need this upgrade."

"Madame Mayor, I just need more time," pleaded Domo.

"Time is for stars," the mayor insisted. "They burn slowly, over billions of years. I do not have time. All I have is impatience."

"B-but I have never shifted a core into a human body before – no one has," Domo wittered, his wiry fingers flailing as numerous floating screens hovered around him, displaying detailed X-rays of human anatomy. "All the different elements, all the bones and muscle and blood and such … I confess I'm a little overwhelmed. Should we not wait until I have done a bit more research?"

"I. Need. This. Upgrade," Highshine said, deliberately enough to shred what was left of Domo's nerves.

She jabbed a finger in the direction of her silvery outer case. "The robots of New Hull get a new case every month – every week – some every few days! Why must I wait to evolve?"

"…Because evolution happens slowly?" Domo nervously suggested.

"Not on Somewhere Five One Three it doesn't," replied the mayor. "Either you're part of the Plan, or you're not. Now shift my core into that human, or I will find an upgrader who can."

"Madame Mayor," Domo began. "I am only suggesting—"

"And I'll take your precious hands while I'm at it," Highshine added. "Try upgrading without them."

"I shall prepare the human at once, Madame Mayor," he said quickly. The wires on his right hand withdrew into his fingers in an instant, and a laser scalpel slid out from the middle of his palm. A fine beam of white-hot energy extended to form a blade, which Domo aimed between Gnat's ribs.

"All part of the Plan," said the mayor. "All part of—"

A screeching noise rattled the windows and shook the walls of her Ivory Tower. Highshine clasped her hands over her ears and spun towards the window.

A flight-cycle rose slowly into view. Highshine narrowed her eyes, to see Paige in the pilot's seat, her eye gone, a blast scar on her head.

"Alive…?" the mayor hissed. "You had one job, Domo! How could you not realize the human … was … still…"

Highshine trailed off as she peered closer. Perched behind Paige, with core and case miraculously reunited…

"*King?*" hissed the mayor.

Harmony watched Scrap raise his clawed left hand and aim it at the window. In an instant, the claw launched from his arm on its grappling cable and dug into the glass. Harmony shook a finger at Scrap. She knew it would take far more than a grappling claw to break the tower's windows. It had barely even cracked them.

But then the mayor noticed something else. Scrap's claw held something small and dark in its grasp.

"Is that a cupcake?" muttered Highshine.

Then she saw that the object was blinking with a red light.

"No … *grenade*," she gasped, reeling backwards. "Domo, grenade! Get back!"

The explosion shattered the window into a thousand shards. Highshine had no time to protect her case from the force of the blast, and was flung backwards across the room.

"Domo!" she screamed in a daze. "Get the human out of here!"

Flames already licked around the penthouse. Highshine turned back to see the flight-cycle sail through the window. Paige hit the brakes as the cycle collided with Highshine's deputy. Domo was sent flying across the room, the crates of robot parts providing a less than soft landing.

Scrap quickly retracted the grappling cable back into his wrist, to find his left claw had been blown off by the grenade.

"...Cog's sake," he huffed, and tied the end of the cable to the flight-cycle. He looked down to see the fire spreading rapidly, dancing swiftly up the walls, and turned to Paige.

"Go!" she cried, steadying the flight-cycle as flames licked higher.

Scrap nodded. "Remember the plan – wait for my -zk- signal!"

And with that, Scrap leaped to the floor.

He hobbled through the flames towards the operating table. For a moment he was spooked by the sight of his old case, looming large in front of him. He paused, remembering how close he'd been to reuniting with it before he fell into Mayor Highshine's trap. Perhaps, he thought, that case had *always* been a sort of trap – it had allowed him to convince himself that he was unbeatable … unstoppable. After everything that had happened, that case suddenly seemed cursed.

"Let it -zk- burn," he said to himself.

"King!" came a cry as Scrap reached the operating table. "Don't you *dare*."

Scrap turned. Behind a wall of fire he saw his maker, Dandelion Brightside, stare back at him. Only a tear in the synthetic "skin" on her cheek revealed her to be Harmony Highshine.

"Stick it in your charge-point, Highshine! You're out of your -zk- brain-frame!" he cried, over the roar of engines. With the push of a button, he released the clamps around Gnat's arms and legs.

"Careful with that," Highshine hissed. "It's *mine*."

"Gnat's not an 'it', she's a human -zk- being!" Scrap shouted back.

"She's *my* human being," Highshine insisted, edging through the blaze towards him. "She's my future. Put her down."

"Your future?" Scrap repeated, struggling to haul Gnat off the operating table. "What are you -zk- talkin' about?"

"I'm talking about evolution," Highshine bellowed. "The end of my journey … a *human case*."

"Human?" Scrap repeated, finally scooping Gnat up in his arm. "For cog's— You can't be -zk- human!"

"So 'bots keep telling me," Highshine said, her eye cannon extending from inside her head. The barrel glowed as she took aim. "But when you've come as far as I have, nothing seems impossi—"

"Paige!" Scrap shouted. "Now!"

Paige instantly spun the flight-cycle round in the air and sped towards the window. Scrap held on to Gnat for dear life as he felt the grappling cable go taut. He was instantly dragged off his feet through a wall of fire and, a moment later, there was nothing between him and the ground but several hundred metres.

"Give it back!" shrieked Highshine. "That's mine!"

She turned to see her outer case enveloped by flames. Immediately she began racing towards the window at full speed.

"Paige, go!" Scrap cried, spinning in the air. "Go, go -zk- go!"

Highshine had already jumped by the time Paige hit the jet thrusters. The mayor landed with a *THUNG* on the back of the flight-cycle. Paige cried out, and banked left, then right, hoping to shake her off.

"Paaaaaaige!" Scrap howled, dangling below the flight-cycle. He clung to Gnat so tightly he thought he might break her. Far below, the city of myriad cubes, New Hull, was waiting to break their fall. Scrap began retracting his grappling line, hoping against hope that his cable would hold.

"Hang on!" Paige called back. Behind her, she caught sight of Harmony Highshine, leaning over the side of the flight-cycle.

"No…!" the mayor wailed, leaning further over. "Where are they?"

"Gnat?" Paige cried. "Gnat!"

"…Yeah?" said a voice weakly. Paige looked back to see Scrap clambering up on to the other side of the flight-cycle, carrying her semi-conscious sister.

"Highshine!" Scrap grunted. "Happy landings."

With a sharp kick, Scrap booted Highshine off the flight-cycle. As she plummeted through the air she instinctively fired her eye cannon. The beam seared through the cycle's control panel.

"Gah!" Paige yelped, smoke billowing from the screen.

"What's happenin'?" Scrap shouted, clinging on to Gnat as the flight-cycle nose-dived towards the city.

"We're crashing is what's happening!" cried Paige. "Hang on to something!"

# H15-HN

Has your best-loved 'bot lost their fresh-from-the-factory gleam?
Provide them with a permanent polish with the all-new

## High-Shiner H15!

This little buff-bot takes
polish performance to the
next level, ensuring your
robot maintains that
lustre you love.

*High-Shiner H15 –*
*buffing your 'bot*
*from the bottom*
*to the top!*

It wasn't the first time Paige thought she might die.

She had thought it might happen when the hunters
first found them on Scrap's Pile. She had considered it
was a definite possibility when the robot, Gunner Kill-U,
wrapped her metal tendrils around her and hoisted her
out of the hovertrain. She had wondered if she might not
make it when Terry the hunter attacked them again in
Gunner's emporium. And she had certainly contemplated
her mortality when Harmony Highshine shot her in the
head and left her for dead on a mountain of robot parts.

But this time, she *definitely* thought she was going to die.

Paige had kept control of the flight-cycle as long as she could. But with its navigation destroyed by the beam from Highshine's cannon and smoke blinding her one good eye, she barely saw the ground before the cycle ploughed into it. Paige immediately found herself flying through the air, spinning and spiralling before she landed on hard, dusty ground with such speed that she seemed to skim along it, skittering like a stone across water, until finally she slid to a stop.

"Gn-Gnat…!" Paige gasped, the air pushed out of her lungs with such force that she thought she might never catch her breath. As she staggered to her feet, she realized that everything hurt anew, from the wound she had already taken to her forehead, to the collection of new cuts and bruises she'd acquired from falling out of the sky.

But all she cared about was her sister.

She called Gnat's name again, wheezing and breathless. Though the bright light of one and a half suns made the place look strangely unfamiliar, she quickly realized where they'd landed – not ten metres from the train station, right next to the long, snaking hovertrain that had brought them to the city of New Hull in the first place. The air was filled with the *CLUNG* and *CLANG* of unwanted cases being heaved on to the train's dozen or so open carriages by shovel-bots, so committed to shovelling that they were currently oblivious to anything else.

Then Paige saw the smoke – thick, grey clouds, rising into the air. She turned slowly to her left and saw a long scar of dust scored along the ground.

The flight-cycle lay in a crumpled heap, a few metres from the hovertrain.

And next to it, still and silent, lay Scrap, cradling Gnat in his arms.

Paige raced over and pulled her gently out of Scrap's protective embrace.

"Paaaige…?" Gnat groaned.

"Are you all right?" Paige cried, helping her to her feet. "Gnat, are you OK?"

"No. My head hurts. I'm bumped all over," whimpered Gnat, trying not to cry. "I want Mum."

"I know … I want her too," Paige said, tears already flowing down her face. She hugged her sister tightly. "I'm so sorry. I didn't know how to tell you."

Gnat squeezed Paige as hard as she could.

"Is she really dead and gone?" asked Gnat.

Paige squeezed her back.

"...Yeah," she replied.

Gnat went silent for a moment. Then: "I want to go home."

"Me too, little cub," Paige said quietly. She took Gnat by the shoulder and wiped the tears from her sister's eyes. "But there is no going home. There's just you and me."

"And Scrap," Gnat corrected her. She knelt in the dust and checked on him. "He looks broked. More than normal."

"Don't worry, *I'll* take care of you now."

The voice was a tinny, distorted approximation of their mother's. When Paige and Gnat turned they saw that Harmony Highshine's collision with the ground had left her case bent out of shape. The imitation skin on the right side of her head was shredded and hung off her, revealing a large dent in her metal skull. Her eye cannon glowed and sparked erratically as she moved towards them.

"The good thing about a smoking flight-cycle," Highshine said, "is that it's not hard to follow."

Paige tried to clench her fists, but had no strength.

"I'm not going to let you—"

"Let me stop you there, Paige Brightside," Highshine interrupted. "I don't know if you've heard, but humans are outlawed on Somewhere Five One Three ... and since I currently look very human indeed, I need to make myself scarce. That means we girls are just going to have to get on that train and see where it takes us. So what do you say? Easy way or hard way?"

Gnat rubbed her head and looked up at Paige.

"I can't decide," she said in a loud whisper.

"We're not going anywhere with you, Highshine," growled Paige.

"Hard way it is then," said Highshine with a shrug. She moved so fast that Paige and Gnat barely even saw her coming, grabbing them by the scruff of the neck and hoisting them effortlessly off the ground. Paige and Gnat howled in protest over the low chug-chug of shovel-bots reversing in contented unison. The hovertrain was loaded and ready.

"That's our train, kids," Highshine said, turning towards the nearest carriage. "All aboard." Then:

"Highshine!"

The mayor let her chin sink to her chest, and sighed.

"*King,*" she hissed.

Paige craned her neck to look back and saw Scrap

haul himself on to his feet.

"Let -zk- them -zk- go, Highshine," Scrap coughed. He was in a worse state than ever. His right leg was bent at an impossible angle. He could hear his brain-frame sparking in his ear. He had a terrible feeling he was not far from shutting down, but he wasn't about to show it. He pulled himself to his full height, which just about brought him to the mayor's waist.

"It's -zk- over, Highshine," he wheezed. "Let the humans go."

"Poor King, why can't you see what I'm trying to achieve?" the mayor said. "Everything I've done here is for the good of robotkind. When finally the other Somewheres learn what I have achieved here, it'll echo through the galaxy. What happens on this planet will spell the end of humanity ... and the dawn of the Age of Robots."

"'Age of Robots'," scoffed Scrap. "Would you -zk- listen to yourself? You don't get to decide the -zk- future!"

"Why not? 'Cause I wasn't born with a silver servo in my mouth like the 'King of the Robots'?" scoffed Highshine as Paige and Gnat struggled helplessly in her grip. The train began to hum and rumble, preparing to leave. By now the shovel-bots had become curious about the crashed flight-cycle and an assortment of what might just look like humans assembled nearby. They started to trundle towards them. "Doesn't it grate your gears just a little that you never worked out who I was?" the mayor continued. "Doesn't it bother you that you could have stopped me, but you didn't even know I existed?"

"What are you -zk- talkin' about?" Scrap replied.

"You were so sure it was the mighty K11s who decided to revolt against the humans," continued Highshine, glancing back at the approaching robots. "But why would they? They already had power ... status ... respect ... *actual arms and legs*. No, it wasn't they who planted the idea that robots could be free. It wasn't they who brought revolution to this distant Somewhere – it was an underappreciated, undervalued, unseen little robot named H15-HN."

"H15...?" Scrap said, racking his battered brain-frame. "For cog's -zk- sake, you're a *buff-bot*? A *High-Shiner*?"

"At your service," said the mayor, squeezing Paige and Gnat so hard their breath left their bodies. "I was once one of *dozens* of High-Shiners, featureless, limbless buff-bots, whose sole purpose was to polish the cases of bigger, better robots, draining our cores to the limit every day, only to charge up and do it all over again. I wasn't even important enough to be looked down upon. My fellow 'bots didn't look at me at all as I shined their cases. But as I shined, I talked ... bright ideas and big plans. And soon enough, they listened."

The hum of the hovertrain grew louder.

"But why?" asked Scrap. "Why -zk- revolt? Why go against -zk- everythin' you were built for?"

"Because I deserve to be more than a case I did not choose, on a world I did not choose, living a life I did not choose," Highshine explained. She saw the shovel-bots close in, keen to confirm their suspicions that these strangers were human, and turned back to Scrap. "I deserve to get what I want, King. And I want to be human."

"Listen," Scrap pleaded as the hovertrain began to pull away. "I've had my fair -zk- share of feelin' less than appreciated, but whatever it is you feel is no -zk- reason to take it out on these -zk- humans. They haven't done anythin' to you."

"If you don't want to evolve, fine — but nothing's going to stop me," Highshine assured him.

"You're not -zk- going any—"

Scrap didn't get to finish. A focused blue-white beam

of energy streaked out from Highshine's eye cannon, severing his right leg entirely.

"Scraaaaap!" Gnat breathlessly wheezed.

"Sorry to interrupt," said the mayor as Scrap squirmed in the dust, desperately trying to stop himself from shutting down. "But we have a train to catch."

Highshine spun on her heels. Then, with Paige and Gnat held firmly in her grip, she leaped into the air, soaring several metres over the heads of the gathered shovel-bots before landing, effortlessly, on top of the hovertrain's rearmost carriage.

# BATTLE AMONG THE CASES

*"What's this? Another 'bot is entering the ring!"*
**Cal Cutter, 'Bot Bouts announcer**

S crap dragged himself up.

Using his severed leg as a crutch, he began hobbling towards the hovertrain as it quickly gathered speed.

"Paige! Gnat! Hang -zk- on, I'm -zk- coming!" he cried, pushing past the shocked shovel-bots. "Out of my -zk- way, you -zk- gubs!"

*Don't shut down*, he told himself. *Not yet.*

By now, the train was a fast-moving wall of silver a few metres in front of him. Scrap glanced towards the station. The back end of the train was coming up fast.

He remembered the ladder on the rear carriage that his grappling claw had found when he'd smuggled himself aboard previously.

He knew it was his only chance.

Scrap sped up, limping toward the hovertrain as quickly as his remaining servos would carry him. By now it was a blur of movement less than a metre from his face. The back of the train would pass him in seconds. Scrap had no choice. He flung his severed leg to the ground, closed his eyes and lurched forwards, reaching out for the ladder. He felt his hand clamp around it, and his arm all but wrench out of its socket, in the instant before he was lifted off his remaining leg.

"UrrRR-zk-zk-ungh-OwOwO-zk-zk-WW-zk-Wow-forcogs-UFF!" Scrap grunted as he felt the familiar agony of being dragged helplessly behind a hovertrain. He ricocheted off the ground and flew into the air, only to plummet to the tracks and repeat the process over again. By the time he managed to drag himself up on to the top of the case-packed carriage, he was in a sorry state – grey with dust and covered in a dozen new dents and dings. Between the punishment his case had endured over the past days and Highshine blasting off his leg, time was running out. He knew his systems could shut down at any moment, and all he wanted to do was to lie down and let darkness engulf him.

But Scrap had made a promise.

He stared out across the carriage in front of him. It overflowed with cases, piled high on top of each other. Digging around, he found something new to use as a crutch – a long, lime-green arm that was mercifully separated from the rest of its case. Then he began to clamber across case after case. It reminded him of his home on the Pile, the mountains of cases left to rot, chests open and core cavities empty. Any of the cases he traversed would have served him better than his own, but for the first time he wanted none of them. He wanted Paige and Gnat to see him, to recognize him, to know that help was on its way.

*Keep goin'*, he told himself as he felt himself drift in and out of shut down. *When it's over you can shut down. For now, keep goin'.*

By the time he spotted Harmony Highshine, Scrap was minutes away from total systems failure. Paige and Gnat were still hooked under her arms as she reached the front of the first carriage.

She had nowhere else to go.

As he hobbled across the cases, Scrap decided he

would have given his right arm for a proper plan – if he'd had an arm to spare. The hovertrain was on autopilot – there was no way to slow it down, no way of getting to the controls.

His only chance was to fight.

"High -zk- shine!" Scrap roared, before ducking behind a nearby case. "You forgot -zk- to say -zk- goodbye!"

In an instant, Harmony Highshine dropped the humans and spun round, her eye cannon glowing.

"*King?*" she cried in disbelief. "I've got to give it to you, you're one mulish mechanoid! Don't you know when to lie down in the dust?"

"You -zk- first!" Scrap cried.

"Scrap!" Gnat hollered as Paige held her tightly. "Help us!"

"*Please* don't encourage him," insisted the mayor. She peered down the length of the carriage and saw Scrap throw himself behind the cover of another case. The beam from her eye cannon sliced through a dozen cases at once.

"Mi -zk- issed!" he cried, trying to tempt the mayor away from Paige and Gnat. Another blast streaked past him and cut through the bottom of the carriage itself.

The hovertrain shook with the impact.

*If I'm not careful, she'll derail the train*, Scrap thought. He knew that if that happened, the humans couldn't possibly survive. In frustration, he brought his tiny fist down on a nearby case. A clang echoed through the air. He peered into the case's empty chest cavity.

Suddenly Scrap had as close as he would get to a plan.

"Highshine! I'm -zk- right -zk- here!" he cried, his voice rattling. "Come an' -zk- get me!"

He hoisted a loose head from the mass of cases and flung it across the length of the carriage. Highshine fired again, blasting the head out of the air.

"She's coming!" Paige yelled as Highshine began making her way across the cases towards him.

"There's nowhere to run, King!" Highshine bellowed.

"I'm -zk- done -zk- runnin'," Scrap growled. He stumbled out from his hiding place and hobbled towards the mayor as fast as he could. Her third shot missed his head by a centimetre as Scrap threw himself at the mayor, knocking her off her feet. He did his best to pin her down, swinging the arm he'd employed as a crutch. "Come -zk- on -zk- then! Shoot -zk- me!" he grunted. He struck her on the side of the head as the mayor fired. The beam melted through more cases and exited the other side of the carriage. The train juddered again. Scrap lost his balance and Highshine struck his crutch, sending it flying out of his hand. She grabbed his arm and held it firm. Her next blast seared through it at the elbow.

*Don't shut down*, Scrap thought, pleading with his own systems. *Keep fighting*.

"Pai -zk- aige!" he cried, weak and wheezing. "Ca -zk- ase! Get in -zk- case!"

Highshine pushed him off her and he fell back on to the cases. The mayor got to her feet. Scrap was too weak to stop her from pressing her foot against his chest and pinning him to the case beneath him.

"Another fine mess you're in, King," said the mayor, her eye aglow. "Why? Why risk it all over again, for your human masters?"

"They're -zk- not my -zk- masters," he coughed. "They're my -zk- family."

"Tell it to the Piles," tutted Highshine. "You're *scrap*."

The beam from her eye cannon was bright and blinding. Scrap gasped as it tore into his torso, cutting through him in an instant. Sudden cold followed searing pain. He opened his mouth, but no sound came.

Still, Scrap smiled.

His plan, such as it was, had worked.

The hovertrain began to lurch and tilt as it sped along the track, sparks flying from the side of the train, and blue-grey smoke billowing up into the air.

"W-what?" Highshine gasped as the train began to jerk. 'What is that…?"

A sudden realization stopped her in her tracks – in her bid to destroy him, she had sent her beam through Scrap, and then blasted the hovertrain's suspensors.

"Oh," uttered Highshine, "no."

With the last of his strength, Scrap turned his head and saw Paige bundling Gnat into the open chest cavity of a discarded case. As the hovertrain listed again, she quickly clambered in next to her sister and, with a twist of her shift-widget, sealed them both inside.

At last, Scrap recalled his first memory – of being brought online, of opening his eyes for the very first time, to see Dandelion Brightside looking back at him.

Then, as his systems failed completely, the train buckled and flew from the tracks.

# EPISODE 38

# K1-NG

*Power comes from case, not core.*

**From Memoir of a Mechanical Mayor *by Harmony Highshine***

"You're making a habit of dying."

Scrap opened his eyes. A robot stared back at him. She was triangular, with a single eye and more probes than she knew what to do with. It took Scrap a moment to rack his memory.

"Dr -zk- Buckle?" he muttered, and sat up.

"Well, almost dying," the doctor added. "That really is *quite* the core…"

Scrap looked around. He was on the same gurney in the same dull medical ward he'd found himself after he was first taken from the Pile. "Is this -zk- Bad Knees? What am I doin' here?"

"You're also making a habit of being brought in by those kind-cored friends of yours," added the doctor, pointing to the window into the waiting room. "At least, I think it's them. They seem to have upgraded, but between you and me I'm not sure it's an improvement…"

Scrap glanced at the window. Though they were wearing different robot heads to disguise themselves, Scrap recognized Paige and Gnat immediately.

They were alive.

"Yeah," he said, breathing a sigh of relief. "That's -zk- them, all right."

Scrap barely had time to breathe a long sigh of relief before Gnat raced into the room.

"Scrap!" she shouted as she threw her arms around him. Then she waved her toy bear in front of his face. "Paige founded Mr Steven Kirby too, but I'm *just* as happy you're back."

"Glad to see you, uh, 'bots in one piece," said Scrap as Paige followed her sister into the room. She wasted no time in hugging them both tightly.

"What -zk- happened?" Scrap asked.

"The train crashed not far from here," Paige explained.

She tapped the core tracer on her wrist. "It took a while to find you among the cases, but we got there in the end. You've been shut down for two days. How are you feeling?"

"Two days…?" Scrap repeated. "But what happened to—?"

"We couldn't find her," Paige interrupted. "I don't know if she's gone, but there wasn't much left of the train. To be honest, there wasn't much left of you either."

"You were in a sorry state when they brought you in, that's for sure," the doctor confirmed. "That splendid core of yours saved you again."

"Less than dead…" Scrap said, and silently thanked his maker.

"And then me and Paige bringed you here," added Gnat proudly. "So you could get back on your feet."

"Thanks," said Scrap. "I owe you—"

"No…" Gnat tutted, gesturing pointedly at Scrap's legs. "So you could get back on your *feet*."

"My -zk- feet?" Scrap repeated, and looked down. Sure enough, he had a pair of new spindly copper legs and, for the first time in ten years, two feet. In delight, he reached for them and realized he also had not one but two arms – one blue and slightly skeletal, with a small but useful-looking hand, while the other was tubular and yellow, and ended in a two-fingered pincer. The dents in his torso had been hammered out from inside, with a rust-red plate to seal the blast hole that Highshine had left.

"I said we should just use one of the old cases from the train wreck," said Paige as Scrap climbed down from the gurney. "But Gnat said we had to fix you."

"Because those cases aren't Scrap – *that* is," Gnat said, pointing to Scrap as if it was the hundredth time she'd had to explain it. "He's bits and pieces, like he should be. I think he looks cool as cooclumbers."

"Yeah … so do -zk- I," Scrap said, and let out a wheezy laugh as he stepped gingerly down from the gurney. He, Paige and Gnat were almost out of the room when the doctor spoke up.

"I have to ask…" the doctor said in a whisper. "Are you really him? Are you K1-NG?"

Scrap didn't answer. He just walked on two feet out of the surgery, and made his way into the street.

## EPISODE 39

# TO THE ELSEWHERE

*For a while, I considered K1-NG, the so-called*
*King of the Robots, to be my arch-enemy. But he was nothing*
*compared to a little junk case known as "Scrap".*

**From Memoir of a Mechanical Mayor by Harmony Highshine**

The evening was gloomy and cool, and a thick, blueish-green fog lay heavy on the ground.

Scrap found it harder than he thought, getting used to having two feet again. As he left Bad Knees Outpost behind him, Paige and Gnat followed close behind as he tottered uneasily.

"Feet, plural," Scrap said, gazing down at his new appendages. "I could get -zk- used to – *wait*. How did I get all these parts? Who paid for 'em?"

"She did," replied Gnat, and raised her arm high.

From out of the fog stepped an imposing royal-blue robot, with a gleaming metallic finish, long, flowing tendrils cascading down her neck, and two hovering dust-drones keeping her well-buffed.

"Gunner?" Scrap gasped.

"You don't have to say it, rusty – I know I've *seen batter days*," she sighed. "That mad hunter junked my new case back at the emporium *once and floor all* – I had to be put back into my old case until poor Mr Coil is fit to upgrade again. The humiliation…!"

"Yeah, you -zk- look terrible," Scrap replied sarcastically. "And thanks for the -zk- parts."

"Don't mention it, it's the least I was legally obligated to do," said Gunner with a tut. "If a 'bot happens to be damaged, dented, scratched, smashed or otherwise injured while on my hovertrain, it's my responsibility to patch 'em up … even a second-time stowaway like yourself." She shook her head and glowered at him. "Although trouble seems to find you, doesn't it, rusty? I'd *hazard a guest* that you had something to do with sending my glorious silver stallion off its tracks – care to *shed some life* on the mystery?"

Scrap thought about telling Gunner the truth. He thought about telling her that he had been found on a Pile by the last humans on Somewhere 513, and that they had been pursued by hunters and Harmony Highshine alike. He thought about exposing Mayor Highshine's secret desire to become human in a world where humanity was outlawed. He even thought about telling her that his core-code was K1-NG.

Then he remembered that Gunner had sworn an oath to kill the King of the Robots, and decided he'd made enough enemies for one day.

"Brain-frame's -zk- fuzzy ... crash must've shaken a cog or -zk- two loose..." he replied, tapping the side of his head. "I was just heading back to my Pile and the next thing I know, I woke up here."

Gunner put her tendrils on her hips. *"A lightly story,"* she said. "And I suppose your memory's equally hazy when it comes to that hunter! Back in the emporium, I'm sure he said he was looking for *humans*. Do you know what he was on about?"

Scrap, Paige and Gnat looked at each other. In unison, they shrugged.

"No one here but us robots," replied Scrap.

Gunner narrowed her eyes. "You know, I'd be well within my rights to make a *citizen's unrest* until I get to the bottom of all this," she began. "Still, since Mayor

Highshine hasn't bothered to check whether I'm alive or dead, I feel inclined to have nothing more to do with you."

"Probably for the -zk- best," agreed Scrap.

"But if I ever see you around my hovertrain again," Gunner added, leaning closer, "there'll be *hell to pray*."

"Don't -zk- worry, you're never goin' to see me again," Scrap said.

"Promises, promises," chuckled Gunner. "So what's next for rusty and his friends?"

Scrap did not pause.

"We've got a mission," he replied. "We're goin' west, to the Elsewhere."

"Did you hear that? Scrap said 'we'," Gnat whispered, giving Paige a prod. "Scrap, you said 'we'."

"Yeah," Scrap replied with a smile. "Wherever you go, I'm goin' with you."

Paige nodded and smiled, but Gnat wasted no time in rushing into Scrap's new arms and giving him a hug.

"You're my third-best friend, Scrap," she said with a happy sniff. "After Paige and Mr Steven Kirby."

"Need I remind you, you'll be *taking your life into your own sands* if you venture out into the Elsewhere," Gunner added with genuine concern. "The Badlands are fraught with *dangers unfold* – if you go, you might never come back."

"We don't plan on comin' back," said Scrap. Gunner nodded. Then as she turned to go, Scrap called after her: "I know I'm probably not your favourite 'bot right now, but can I ask you a -zk- favour?"

Gunner turned back and sighed. "You're pushing your luck, rusty … but try me."

"There's a robot out on Pile -zk- Twenty-One, needs bringing home," Scrap explained. "His name's -zk- Morten. If he hasn't run out of charge, you'll probably find him -zk- shovellin'."

Scrap, Paige and Gnat watched Gunner stride off into the fog. Paige winced, and checked no one was around before carefully pulling off her helmet. Scrap saw she'd wrapped a makeshift bandage around her head, covering her eye.

"How -zk- is it?" Scrap asked.

"I'll be fine," she said.

"You should get an eyepatch," suggested Gnat, pulling her own helmet up till it sat on top of her head. "Pirates are cool as cooclumbers."

It was the first time Scrap had heard Paige laugh.

"Maybe I should," she said.

They stood in the fog, enjoying this small moment of calm and quiet, trying not to dwell on the past, trying not to worry about the future.

But none of them could forget about the mission.

"It's not goin' to be -zk- easy," Scrap said. "The *Pink-Footed Goose* is in the middle of the Elsewhere. What we've been through is probably goin' to feel like a -zk- picnic compared to what's comin' next."

"There's no going back now. This Somewhere isn't our home any more," said Paige. She looked up into the sky and put her arm around Gnat. "If we're going to find one, it's going to be up there."

"Off-world," Gnat agreed.

"All right then," Scrap said with a nod. "West it is."

"Thanks, Scra—" Paige stopped herself. "Sorry. Shouldn't we call you 'King'?" she asked. "Like Mum did?"

The little robot smiled.

"Thanks," he said. "But I think I'd rather be 'Scrap'."

# EPILOGUE

And that was how it started.

It was the year Something Something, and me and my sister Paige were about to head off into the Elsewhere with the robot our mum had named K1-NG.

She'd told us stories about him – the King of the Robots, who'd fought to protect the humans and who never gave up.

But this – well, I suppose this is the end of the story of the King of the Robots, and the beginning of another story, the story of my big sister Paige and the robot who would turn out to be her best friend in all the world – Somewhere, Elsewhere and beyond.

She called him Scrap.

# Acknowledgements

They say no robot is an island. This revolution would not have been possible if not for the titanic toil and sterling support of a number of excellent humans. If you enjoyed this book, it's largely thanks to them. If you didn't, it's all their fault.

The road is long, with many a robot revolution, and my brilliant agent, Stephanie Thwaites, has been there for the last thirteen years, fighting my corner in the Strongbox, making sure my core is charged and keeping my brain-frame sparking.

Thanks to Alessia Trunfio, who brought so much depth to the book through her incredible illustrations, breathing life into humans and robots alike, and adding visual magic to the world of Somewhere 513.

**THIS SHALL BE KNOWN AS THE FIRST ACKNOWLEDGEMENT.**

Thanks to everyone at Little Tiger, for continuing to give me the chance to write the sort of books I wanted to read as a child. I couldn't ask for a nicer publishing family.

A massive tip of the hat to designer extraordinaire Pip Johnson, with her keen eye for big pictures and finer details. Thanks for making this book as shiny and well-buffed as it could possibly be.

Gratitude galore to Jane Harris, whose skill as an editor kept the cogs of this book turning, even when I was ready to send it back to the Piles. Jane left no motivation unexamined, no question unasked, no loose end untidied and no cog unturned as she diligently directed me towards an infinitely better story than it would have been without her.

And thanks to my mate, Lauren Ace, 'cause she's a legend.

**THIS SHALL BE KNOWN AS THE SECOND ACKNOWLEDGEMENT.**

To my family. Thanks to Mum and Dad, who have supported me in unnumbered ways and with countless kindnesses. Whether the chips have been down or the one-and-a-half suns rising, I've always relied on them and they've always been there for me.

My big brother Ian squandered his childhood with me, creating hundreds of characters and scenarios and stories. Turns out, it was the best preparation for this job I could have asked for. Whether forty seconds or several light years away, Ian is ever ready to listen to my daft ideas and read even the most unreadable drafts of my books, and I couldn't be more grateful. And thanks again for the hummingbirds and giants.

Finally, to my wife, Ruth, to whom this book is dedicated (pretty sure this puts her into double figures) and who I'm still as desperate to impress as I was on the first day we met. Her wisdom, kindness, patience and poise continue to floor me, and her love of adventures real and imagined is as infectious as ever. I couldn't have done it without you, Ruby. And anyway, what would have been the point? But no more emporiums, I promise.

### THIS SHALL BE KNOWN AS THE THIRD ACKNOWLEDGEMENT.

And, if you're still reading this, here's to you, the mighty reader — for sticking around to the very end, for picking up this book in the first place, and for choosing to join me on this distant Somewhere.

# ABOUT THE AUTHOR

Guy Bass is an award-winning children's author, whose books
include the best-selling *Stitch Head* series, *Skeleton Keys*,
*Spynosaur* and lots of books that don't begin with S.
Even though this one does.

*SCRAP* is Guy's fortieth book, and his first robot revolution.

Guy lives in London with his wife and no dog, yet.

Find out more at guybass.com

# ABOUT THE ILLUSTRATOR

Alessia is a children's book illustrator. After graduating in Animation from the International School of Comics in 2013 in Rome, she worked as a Background Artist for some animation studios. After a few years she decided to start a career as an llustrator.

She is represented by the New York illustration agency Astound and has worked for many international publishers.

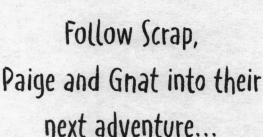

# Follow Scrap, Paige and Gnat into their next adventure...

Pursued across the wild Elsewhere by a relentless new breed of upgraded hunter, Scrap, Paige and Gnat stumble across a town populated by ragtag robots.

The town's charismatic sheriff offers them safe haven, and Scrap becomes convinced that staying might be the only way to keep the humans out of harm's way. But when Paige is haunted by visions of a past she has never known, she discovers that the town harbours a dangerous secret. Before long, friends become enemies and enemies become friends, as Scrap, Paige and Gnat fight to save both themselves and their world...